London Falls on Everest

By

Reneé Nicole

It Started with an E-mail Series #1

Edited by: Hannah Morin

Copyedit: Catherine Wiley

Cover Design: Katelin Spector

Proofread & Formatting: Lili Booth

Published by: Dream It. Plan It. Grow It.

About the Book

London Isle started from the bottom and is now the successful small town real estate developer that she always wanted to be. But she is still spending her nights alone. All it takes is her 'no filter' executive assistant, several bottles of wine, and an email to get London the chance most women would kill for: a date with "The Mountain" himself, superhero, Ezra Everest. But dating a famous superhero comes with a different level of drama and crisis. London finds herself descending into a serious trauma that she thought she had overcome. Now to help Ezra, she must relive her past demons.

****Warning: This is an adult novel for your enjoyment. Adult scenes and action to follow, it is recommended for those ages 18 and up. Enjoy.****

****This novel contains references to suicide and death. Please be advised.****

Dedication

This book is dedicated to my siblings. Because you are the people in my world I couldn't live without. Thank you for being in my corner, always. I love you, with all that I am, plus my whole heart.

Chapter One

I have a powerful belief in manifestation. I know that what goes around, comes around and what you think about, you bring about. So, when I tell you what happened to me next, you should know that it was all in the will of the universe.

I am a small-town girl who decided to invest in land in a rural community. Turns out, I'm really good at it. I managed to turn my four acre purchase of land into a commercial development. This allowed me to make my second purchase of seven acres to develop into a different commercial development. Fast forward to eight years later and now I have made my next purchase of twenty acres to develop. I am on track to keep developing small towns throughout the country. I am proud of myself and if you knew the shit I've had to overcome, you would be proud of me too. But I don't want to tell you my sad 'woe is me' story. I want you to hear my 'happily ever after' story.

It all starts with two bottles of red wine, Amelia, my assistant, who is more like my sister, and an internet search.

Let me explain.

It is 4:15 in the afternoon and Amelia is already pouring us a glass of red wine. We are celebrating my new land purchase of twenty acres to develop with commercial and residential real estate, in another small town in Nebraska.

"London, you did it, another property. I'm going to need my own assistant soon if we keep grinding like this," Amelia points out with a huge smile on her face.

I believe Amelia may be right; we have turned our small operation into a profitable business that crosses state lines.

"Ami, with this purchase you are absolutely right. Getting someone to lighten your load is on the 'to do' list."

Amelia continues to be all smiles at that idea; she only suggested it as a joke, but there was definitely some truth to it.

As she hands me my glass of red, I make a toast. "Congratulations to both of us. Let's drink to vision boards, manifesting, hustle, and never backing down."

As I am about to clink my glass with Ami, she moves her glass back and says, "Nope, we always drink to that. Let's drink to boss bitch vibes, finding men with big dicks, and world domination."

I laugh, look her in the eyes, and say, "I'll fucking drink to that."

About one and a half bottles in, we start to discuss celebrities we would love to date because that is what regular single women do. We talk about the stars like they are untouchable and dream of the chance to touch them. With consent, of course. I am telling Amelia how dating a superhero would be epic and we decide that Captain American, Spiderman, or Superman would be the ultimate catch for me. Because why not? We are just dream-talking and drinking red wine. Red wine always loosens my lips and emotions. And we are mixing up the superhero universes but who cares?

"You know who I have crazy daydream chemistry with?" I say. "That mountain of a man, Ezra Everest. Just yum. I know he dates but is single by choice but what I wouldn't give to climb him. You know he is so charitable too, always giving back to the community. I saw a special on him about what he does for young aspiring actors and women's shelters. I bet he really knows how to please a girl. I would buy him dinner any day, and a mountain too." I am laughing at my own joke; I have absolutely had too much wine. "Get it, Ami, buy him a mountain, because of his name?" I look at her, thinking she may be laughing at my joke. She is not. I thought it was funny.

Before I know it, Amelia has her computer out and I know she can't be working. We are one and a half bottles in and if I am feeling the red wine, I know she is too. But Ami is focused on something on the computer screen, and I can only assume she is watching porn since we just spent the last hour talking about men and how sex would be with a superhero.

"What are you looking for?" I ask while looking at the ceiling, dreaming about sex with stars and my next big land development idea.

Ami mumbles, "I'm sure I can use this thing somehow for the betterment of your lady parts, in a completely legal way, and I am going to find it."

"Find what?" I ask as I throw my legs up on the couch.

"His people."

"Whose people? What people? Ami, are you looking at porn again on the work computer? I told you it messes up the computer and then we have to get the 'over-sharer' from the offsite to help us."

"No. I learned my lesson the last time," she says before shrieking. "OMG, London, I found it! I can't believe it, but I found his people."

"Whose people?" I ask again as I shift my head on the couch to look in her direction. "I thought we were drinking, not working," I tell her as she looks around her computer screen to me.

"I am absolutely not working. I found the email information for Ezra Everest's personal assistant's assistant. See, he has multiple assistants. Obviously."

"Obviously," I state with an eye roll. "I'm sure that is a scam; you can't just find 'his people' on the internet."

"I fucking can find his people on the internet," Ami answers with a scoff as if I have offended her skills. "I found Ezra Everest's people. The one and only, body for days, superhero action movie star, animal-loving, charity-giving, sex god who makes all women, and probably some men, wish they could climb Everest."

"You know what I mean," I mumble as I hear the keyboard clicking. "What are you doing?"

"I am being an amazing fucking assistant and getting you a fucking date with a 'Mountain,'" Amelia says with pure determination in her eyes, before taking a sip of wine. I guess she agrees with my daydream chemistry idea.

"What?" I stumble a bit as I get up and head in her direction. "No, you can't do that. There were a lot of fucks in that sentence."

She laughs. "Right. But I have had just enough wine and the right amount of stalker vibes to do this for you, London. Just you wait."

I add, "I have had just enough wine to agree with you and let you send this email, but it needs to be noted that I think the email address you found is a scam. So, when you get emails for enhancing your penis and sex drive, I will be here to say, 'I told you so.'"

"So noted. Now, pour us another glass, and let's get you a date with the Mountain."

As I watch her fingers fly over the keyboard, I want to know exactly what she is saying. "What's the subject line, Ami? It must be eye-catching if we expect the assistant's assistant to read it."

"I'm thinking. I need more wine," Amelia states just as I am refilling her glass.

"More wine always helps with the creative process. What could possibly go wrong?" I say, my voice dripping with sarcasm.

Amelia is thinking out loud when she says, "It can't say anything about business because the personal assistant wouldn't deal with that. What if it has something to do with giving back to small communities?"

"What? No. That's a lie, and I am not a charity," I say, shocked with the level of excitement I have at sending this spam email.

"Got it. For your eyes only. Urgent. Personal matter for Ezra Everest. Response requested."

"I don't know if he or she will read that. Sounds like spam."

Amelia looks at me like I am out of touch. "When was the last time you didn't open an email that said for your eyes only?" She definitely has a point; I am nosey and so are other people. I believe we have a subject line.

Ami keeps thinking out loud. "We want the first line to be eye-catching, but professional, so that means no nudies or 'date me.'"

I laugh at her nudies comment because she knows I would never have nudes. Not that I am ashamed of my body. I am beautiful with my southern accent, curvy hips, C-cups, and hazel-gray eyes. I work out to keep healthy, not for muscle or show, and I darken my hair so that my eyes will be very noticeable when you look at me. All positives here, but I am your normal woman, with baggage and a bright future. Why would someone with star status like Ezra Everest, movie and TV star, The Mountain himself, be interested in a normal woman like me? Yes, I am successful in my own business community, but it is success in my lane, in my realm, not in Ezra Everest's realm. Oh lord, I am thinking in realms now. I may need to slow down on the wine. But you know, just in case (glass half-full kind of girl here), it is not a spam email.

"I would be short and to the point, because no one reads emails that are really long anymore," I say.

Amelia has a light bulb moment because she says, "You're right."

To whom it may concern:

I hope this email finds you well. This is a dinner invitation to Mr. Ezra Everest from Ms. London Isle. Ms. Isle is a real estate business mogul who has invested in small towns in North Carolina, South Carolina, Georgia, Alabama, and now Nebraska, building commercial and residential properties that are environmentally safe and affordable for working- and middle-class business owners and families. Ms. Isle has been featured in several business articles and won Businesswoman of the Year three years in a row in North Carolina, South Carolina, and Georgia, and most recently won Most Influential Businesswoman in North Carolina. Find an attached image of Ms. Isle. Please reply to this email to schedule the dinner date, time, and location that would work best for Mr. Everest's schedule.

Thank you for your attention. We await your response.

Amelia Corse,

Executive Assistant to London Isle

Isle, LLC

I am reading over Ami's shoulder as she writes this email. "Wait, that makes it seem like I'm asking him out," I say. "Shouldn't it be the other way around?"

Ami remarks, "First, you are a boss, and you can ask a man out. Second, asking him out shows assertiveness, and third, you don't even think this is fucking real, so what do you care?"

"Well, if you're going to send the email make it a good picture you attach," I say, wanting to sound unaffected but also thinking that this would be cool if it worked. Also, maybe I need to go on a date. It has been a while. I am really thinking and trying to recall my last date. The last time I went out with a man was James, and that doesn't count because all we did was bump into each other at the restaurant downtown while I was having dinner alone, and then we came back to my place for a quick fuck. It's never a date with James; he isn't a man to whom I would ever give more of my time or energy than strictly necessary. I shake myself out of that thought in time to hear Amelia.

"I'm not sending him a headshot. I'm sending something less formal where your smile reaches your eyes," Ami states matter-of-factly.

"Send both," I note before she presses send. "Wait, you really sent that? Like really?" I ask as if Ami has ever been a bullshitter. Because she most definitely has been a straight shooter since the day I met her.

"Of course. I feel good about this, and it will end in a positive outcome. As you say, what you think about, you bring about. You know, busy manifesting and all that positive energy shit we say," Amelia states as she logs off the computer and throws my affirmation words back at me. Well, at least I know she is listening when I speak.

With the email gone and us falling back into our normal chatter, we finish our celebration and soon move past our long-shot email. I get Ami an Uber home because we have polished off three bottles of wine and I can barely make it to my own home upstairs. She can't possibly drive. My home is a three-bedroom condo above my office spaces. It's a beautiful space in the downtown area where all the very little action happens. But I love my community. I wasn't born here, but this is where I bought my first property, and this community has taken me in and made this place my home.

I barely get my shoes off before I fall on the bed, in my suit skirt and top, and drift off into a wine-induced sleep.

* * * *

It's three weeks later when I hear a scream coming from Amelia's office. I ran up there because her scream scares the shit out of me and I think she is hurt.

"OMG, Amelia what happened? Do I need to call 9-1-1?"

She waves her hand as she dances in her office. I mean seriously dances, doing the running man, and throwing her hands in the air and waving them while saying, "Don't be dramatic."

"Me, dramatic? You just screamed like someone was trying to kill you and you're doing the running man in, four-inch, yes of course, Christian Dior?"

She is too busy celebrating to listen to me. "Look, OMG, they responded! There's a copy with the personal assistant. This must be a legit email." Ami reads the response to me,

Amelia,

Thank you for reaching out. We have discussed this with Mr. Everest, and he would be delighted to have dinner with Ms. Isle. Please see the attached options for dates, times, and locations, and reply with Ms. Isle's best available time.
Best,
-V

I walk over to look at the email on her computer screen, because really? It is literally signed V. No other letters. I guess when you work for Ezra Everest you can go by one letter.

"This has to be a scam. It was weeks ago when we sent that email," I say to Ami. Amelia is shaking her head. "I know, right, but I knew I shouldn't give up yet. There are actually dates, times, and locations attached to this email. Look, he's in South Carolina the same week as us. You could pick that date. It's not for a few weeks, but at least we will already be spending the month there."

I'm still trying to wrap my head around this response. I cannot believe this is real, so I tell Ami to do her research before committing to this date just to be on the safe side, adding, "I do not want to be catfished." I can't think of anything more embarrassing. I mean, I can, but I don't want to.

Amelia agrees and states, "I will vet the shit out of this and if it's real, I am setting the date."

Chapter Two

After several days of researching and verifying, Amelia comes to me excited. She's confirmed that this date is real. "I've done it," she says with the brightest smile. "You are officially going on a date with a sexy, hot, famous, and available movie star."

I can't believe a night full of red wine led me to a date with Ezra Everest. I haven't felt this excited about seeing a guy in…well, in forever. This is a big change from that fuckboy, James—certainly not an untouchable, handsome movie star. Ezra Everest with the sexy eyes, muscled arms, impeccable talent, and just pure beauty, because that man is beautiful. "I cannot believe this is happening. So, it's legit? He's really going to meet me for a date?"

"Not only is it legit, but you two will be dining at one of the plantations in Charleston, South Carolina, as his team has rented the house to keep the date from the public and tabloids," Ami adds.

"Wow. That makes sense. I don't want to be featured in a tabloid, especially if he turns out to be an ass in real life. Or if I'm awkward at the date and he runs screaming from the room." I just hope my face is saying to Ami excited and not I'm about to puke on the office floor.

As Ami is about to head back out of my office, I stop her. "Wait, I don't know what the fuck to wear and I don't understand fancy table settings. This could go wrong in so many ways."

Ami calmly says, "He's not a royal; you don't need to understand fancy table settings. He would probably appreciate a date with a real woman who won't 'fangirl' all over him, and finding your perfect outfit is what this week will be all about."

"But we have so much work to do," I remind her.

"Don't you worry, I am a multitasking queen. This will work."

Ami leaves to return to her workspace, hopefully to use those epic multitasking skills to make sure that I don't look like a complete loser on this date.

* * * *

After a search through my closet leads me to stress hives and a bottle of vodka, Ami and I hit the internet and local boutiques in search of the perfect outfit. I really don't know if I should wear a dress or jeans. I know the location of the date and what to expect of the setting, but the perfect outfit still escapes me. It takes many days, but because Ami is the best assistant ever, she manages to find the perfect skirt and top combination that says sexy and classy. The sky-blue miniskirt fits me like a glove, doesn't ride up when I walk, makes my legs look eight miles long, and highlights my ass as the perfect lure of 'grab it or slap it.' The grey shirt has thin straps that cling to the edges of my shoulders, a sweetheart neckline, and a crisscross cutout back. This outfit is a wear-no-bra-or-panties kind of outfit and when I put it on, I feel powerful, beautiful, and sexy. I pair the outfit with rose-colored Louis Vuitton's and the color contrast works perfectly. Ezra Everest is about to meet his match.

I manage to relax my nerves with some motivating mirror self-talk and a glass of red wine. It helps to get ready alone, so I don't work myself back up into a ball of nerves. I want to go on this date and show him the cool woman that I am. With my makeup flawlessly applied and hair long down my back with some soft curls, I make my way to the Plantation.

Amelia calls while I am driving to the plantation.

"Hey," I answer the call in the car with a bit of nerves in my voice.

"I called to tell you that you are smart, funny, accomplished, educated, opinionated, and perfect for this date," Ami says. "Do NOT forget that, London. You deserve this chance. It's just a date and if he's an ass, it will be one hell of a story to tell your kids one day."

"Thanks, Ami. You always know how to fill me with good vibes."

"I don't want you doubting yourself. Have fun. Are you close?"

"I think I am. The GPS says six minutes until arrival. I'm going to be on time. I feel like I'm not being mysterious enough by showing up on time, though," I admit to Amelia.

"I'm sure he has had mysterious plenty of times. Being punctual is rare these days when it comes to dating. That will leave an impression." Ami says this with excited confidence.

"I like that. First impressions are everything. I just don't want to appear too fangirl-eager."

"I think you should address that first. Make a 'Hey, wow, you're The Mountain, and you're hotter in person, now let's move past that' kind of comment. Let him know that his movie star status doesn't excuse him from being 'first date judged' like the rest of the men in the world."

I smile widely at Amelia's summary of the first words that should come out of my mouth. "First date judged. That is perfect, Ami." We are both laughing when I take the final turn and make my way down the driveway to the mansion. "Okay. I've got to go. I'm pulling up now. I will do one final makeup check and then go to knock on the door. I will call you after."

Ami huffs, "I will be in your room when you get in tonight. I need every detail."

I am shaking my head as I say, "Bye girl," knowing that Ami will absolutely stick to her word and be in my room when I get back to the condo we're renting while working in South Carolina.

I admire the plantation as it comes into view, from the astonishing grounds to the pristine brickwork, beautiful white columns, and stunning entry door. I take a moment to ponder the beauty from one of our country's most despicable historic periods. I pull past the steps leading to the front door, noticing there are no other cars in front of the mansion. I am just freshening my lipstick in the mirror when there is a soft knock on the window. I am so on edge that I jump, even though the knock was not intended to scare me.

I hear a man's voice outside the running car's window. "Ms. Isle, I will park your car."

Exhaling and trying to slow my heart rate, I look out the window to a smiling face reaching for the door handle. I quickly make sure the car is in park and toss my lipstick back in my bag. I give the valet a nod. As he opens my door, I am secretly grateful that I am in an SUV, since I don't have to worry about flashing the valet—because this skirt is not meant for low seats—or struggling to climb out of a car.

He takes my hand and I accept his assistance getting out of the car while telling him, "The key fob is in the cup holder." Once I'm out of the vehicle, I smooth my skirt. He lets go of my hand and, gets in with a smile and nod, driving my car away.

"No turning back now, London," I say to myself because I am standing in the gravel-filled driveway about to have the first date of most women's—single and maybe not single—

dreams. I say my mantra as I climb the short flight of brick stairs. "Deep breath and let's go, Lo."

I am about to knock on the door when it's opened by a petite round woman. She motions for me to come in. "I will take your bag, Ms. Isle," she says.

I enter and hand over the small clutch that can only hold my ID, lipstick, and cell phone. I don't mind handing over my bag; being technology-free is my favorite kind of relaxation. With my clutch in her hand, she leads me to the foyer where she leaves me with a polite, "Mr. E. will be right in."

Chapter Three

I'm looking at all the history and artwork on the walls when I hear sliding doors open in the distance, footsteps, and then someone clears their throat to get my attention. It feels like a slow-motion turn with a complete toe-to-head intake before our eyes meet—blue to hazel—and there is a pause of appreciation before he takes a step toward me with his hand extended in greeting. He is dressed much more casually than I am, but he still looks extremely nice in his blue jeans, teal button-down shirt with the sleeves rolled up—which does wonders for his eyes— and his Gucci shoes.

"Hi, London. Ezra." He stumbles over his words.

I turn my smile up a notch to see this gorgeous man stumbling over his words like a normal guy meeting a pretty girl. My ankles don't get the message to move forward because when I step forward to take his hand, my ankles wobble and I nearly fall in my sexy-as-fuck—but clearly dangerous—Louis Vuittons, but Ezra catches my hand and elbow to keep me upright. This puts us directly in each other's personal space, and I can feel the electricity running between us. *Yum*, is all I can think.

"I bet all the girls stumble in your presence," I say with a nervous and embarrassed laugh. *Oh, how original, London, I am sure he has heard that a thousand times.* I continue quickly past my not-funny line. "Yes, hey, I'm London, whose ankles appear to be failing at the moment, but I promise I can walk in these shoes, nice to meet you, Ezra."

Now I am rambling. Be cool. Jeez, London. I am still smiling at him, hoping that takes his mind off of my near fall. When I manage to get out of my head enough, I can see his smile has reached his eyes and that he is amused by my rambling and stumbling. He must be processing our closeness, the spark, and our still-entwined hands, because he says, "They're great ankles." I can see the moment he starts yelling at himself in his head over that compliment because he blushes and dips his head slightly. He clears his throat again and says, "It's nice to meet you too. Let's go into the living room; they have a great layout for dinner."

Steadying myself, I say, "That sounds wonderful," and with a bit too much exuberance, I ask, "Is there alcohol?"

He gives a breathy laugh and says, "God yes, what will you have?"

I realize that Ezra Everest is nervous about this date too and that gives me all kinds of butterflies inside.

"I will have vodka with a splash of sparkling water," I say as we both enter the living room, and he heads for the bar set up to the right. I look at the beautiful table arrangements, place settings, candles, and stunning flowers.

I am carefully and elegantly leaning in to smell the flowers when I catch Ezra checking out my legs and following them up to my ass as he pours our drinks. He takes a quick sip of his and then makes another; clearly, he is either in a mental battle to calm himself or looking for a quick exit. The quick exit is a negative thought and I quickly readjust my thinking patterns as he says, "The flowers are beautiful. Are you a woman who loves flowers?"

"Yes, I absolutely am. Give me flowers and you can just about get anything out of me."

"Anything?" Ezra asks with a raised eyebrow.

"Look at you with the dirty mind and flirting out the gate," I say with playfulness in my eyes. "Yes, anything, but I would call myself a 'flower enthusiast.' The flowers have to be special, not your everyday flowers. I like the unique ones. You have to put real effort into sending flowers to me. I like flowers like zinnias, dahlias, birds of paradise, peonies, hibiscuses, anthuriums, and irises. So, I never expect flowers from men, because it can be difficult to impress me with flower choices." James, my last fling, once showed up with a single Gerber Daisy at my door, thinking it would get him into my house unannounced. I accepted the basic flower and then asked him to leave because I was headed to the airport. I wasn't really, but I didn't like him showing up unannounced. I don't know why that thought crossed my mind; I have a real-life superhero in my line of sight. *James fucking who?* I get back to my point with Ezra. "But these are still elegant and beautiful; you can never go wrong with the understated beauty of roses and hydrangeas. They smell great, too. Whoever prepared this room did an outstanding job."

I can see Ezra putting thought into what I just revealed. "It does look really nice," he says as he walks over with our drinks, but adds, "Not as nice as you look, London. I am truly taken aback by your beauty. The picture did not do you justice." At that comment, a blush rushes up my neck and my face nearly splits with my smile.

"Thank you. I can say the same about you. In person, you are beyond orgasmic."

He truly laughs at the compliment. "Beyond orgasmic. Never heard anyone describe me that way."

We are defiantly eye-fucking each other, and I take a drink of my vodka to cool the connection before saying, "Should we get the fangirl moment out of the way?"

"Fangirl?" He looks disappointed, like I am about to go into the 'autograph and tears of joy' mode.

"Not that type of fangirl moment. Just the moment when I say that I've seen your work, though only the action movies. You're talented and congratulations on your success."

He exhales, and I can see his relief. "Thank you. I thought you were going to pull out a camera, and then ask for a photo and autograph. Or, even worse, that you'd turn out to be a stalker type of fan."

"No, I am impressed by all people's level of success. It takes a lot of work, dedication, and resilience to be successful. In your line of work, I imagine the resilience you have to have and the work you put in is all pushed under the rug without the appropriate amount of acknowledgment."

"That's the nicest thing anyone has ever said to me," he says with shock in his voice.

"Well, I'm sorry it took so long to hear that from someone."

"Thanks." He is clearly thrown by my statement because he doesn't add more.

"So, now that we have addressed the elephant in the room. Let's do the awkward first date dance like us normal 'non-movie star' folks do. We already got the memorable entrance with my near fall and word vomit."

I like the sparkle in his eye at my comments. "You did make a hell of a first impression, but it wasn't for either of those reasons."

"Really, what was your first impression?"

"Damn, she is sexy as fuck." We both laugh before he adds, looking me directly in my eyes, "See me."

I know exactly what he is trying to say without him saying it. The life of the famous must be extremely lonely, never knowing who to trust, who your real friends are, who is good for you, and who you need to avoid. We enjoy the entertainment they provide, but we don't really respect the toll it must take for them to provide it.

With the eye contact of this moment, I can sense how exposed he must feel. I want him to know that I will look at him, not at his fame.

"You don't have to worry, Ezra. I'm very observant. I will pay attention to all that you want to show me and still manage to see all that you want to keep hidden." The moment is full of intense 'I want to know you and fuck you' type of passion. So much so that I think he might kiss me, but we haven't even had dinner. I feel like we should do that first, so I inhale audibly and break the tension with one of my random questions. "So, tell me the high point and low point of your day?"

I can see him realizing what I am doing, but instead of losing the connection, he shifts it, taking my hand and leading me to the table, where he pulls out my chair for me to sit and takes his seat across from me.

He doesn't think my question is weird and has no issue with answering. "My low point was having the studio pass on a script I wrote under a pseudonym, and by a long shot my high was walking into that foyer a few minutes ago." I blush at his high point but wonder how he is going to recover from his low. Before I can ask, he says, "Tell me yours."

"Sure. My low point was having to fire my project manager for this South Carolina development I'm working to build. He didn't see my vision; he didn't take me seriously and was half-assing it with getting the contractors to do their jobs. Firing people is always hard and uncomfortable for me."

"As it is with everyone. I'm positive about that," Ezra adds to encourage me to continue.

Nodding my head in agreement, I keep going. "My high point was the moment I realized you would take this date seriously and give me the real Ezra and not the person they show us on TV." I continue even though I know he hasn't asked for an explanation. "I've been single for a while, and no one seems genuine anymore. It's hard for me to tell who deserves my effort and time." I take a sip of my drink and wait to see if he is going to add anything.

"Yes, I will say that when I was approached with this date, I had a different idea, but the 'my ankles work' comment when I met you changed that idea immediately."

"Well, I am glad to hear that, Ezra. My time is irreplaceable, and my efforts always lead to ultimate pleasure," I say without any shame at the sexual innuendo.

"Look who's flirting now, London."

The server comes out to tell us about the meal we will be having and then looks to Ezra for approval. After Ezra gives a slight nod of his head, the server brings back a bottle of

Caymus Napa Valley Cabernet Sauvignon, and after he approves, she opens the bottle and pours a sample into the glass for him to taste. After his taste, he says, "Yes, that will do perfectly." The server pours us both a glass and then disappears.

We make eye contact and raise our glasses in a toast. "To chance email responses," he says.

I laugh at that because he is completely right. Ami sent that email by chance and 'V' responded by chance. "I'll drink to that. Cheers."

It seems like all the stress has been lifted because the conversation flows without pause. He tells me why he is in South Carolina, while I explain the project I am currently eight months into. We talk about his family, and I tell him about Amelia being the only real family I have. I don't want to bring down the evening, so I tell him that my family history is troubled, distant, and non-existent and that I don't want to bring down the vibe of the date. But I promise that I will tell him my story at a more appropriate time. He seems to accept my answer, but I can tell it is not the last time I will hear the question.

We discuss everything from religion to politics to our first sexual experience. By the time dessert comes, we are on the second bottle of wine and drifting into dirty talk. This conversation is heating up my body; it won't be easy to fall asleep without an orgasm tonight. Good thing I brought my vibrator with me on this trip.

Ezra wants to know so much about me, and I can tell he is an active listener throughout the entire conversation. "Tell me your favorite place to be kissed?" he asks.

"In public, so that others will know I am with you," I answer, a knowing look in my eyes because that is not what he meant.

He gives me a smirk before adding, "On your body?"

"You will have to be quite specific with me, Ezra. You will learn that I like to hear exactly what you mean, especially when it comes to dirty talk. I have two places that will guarantee the response you want. In public, the back of my neck, but in private, my pussy."

He does a great job of not overreacting to my response and without losing eye contact—ensuring I see all the heat in his eyes from my response—he takes a drink of his wine.

"Your turn," I say. "Tell me."

"In public, my shoulder. In private, my hip right before you put my cock in your mouth."

"Those are good kissable spots."

"I agree with you, London." I have to cross my legs under the table because I am getting wet from this conversation, and I need some pressure on my pussy. He pushes on. "What's your favorite sexual position?" He clearly heard what I said before because he is specific with his question this time.

"That's a hard one, because it depends on your ability to perform correctly in the position that I want and the size of your cock to get in the spot that I want." I'm making sure my responses are specific to him because I want him to picture us doing these things. "My favorite position is on my back, legs to the side or up in the air and closed together. Or on top riding hard with my hand on the headboard. Can you picture what I mean?" I ask, as if I don't know what I am doing to him.

"Yes, I can picture that perfectly. Thank you. I may use that image later."

"Ah, so you are okay with sex toys and touching yourself, with or without me watching."

"I am okay with all of those, with or without you watching."

"I like that, Ezra."

"Did you bring your vibrator with you to South Carolina?"

"I did. Whether this date went great or horrible, I was going to fuck myself tonight while thinking about your blue eyes, your shoulders, and those big hands that look like they give a great finger fuck."

He smirks and licks his lip while running those sexy long fingers around the rim of his wine glass. "I will come to the image of your sexy as fuck legs in that mini-skirt with those fuck-me heels, that ass that I can tell doesn't have any panties on it tonight, and the fact that your nipples are hard through that shirt just from listening to my words."

"What makes you think I'm not wearing any panties?" I asked with a knowing smile.

"Because that skirt is not made for panty lines."

"You are a very smart man, Everest."

"I like to think so, London Isle."

This conversation has gotten so hot that I don't even realize how close we are leaning into each other until the server comes to take away the desserts. She asks, "Do either of you want coffee or water?" I realize I may need water if I intend to drive home tonight. I smiled up at her and requested black coffee and a water. Ezra requests water too, and she leaves us.

"Have you had too much to drink to remember this date?" I ask him, a bit worried about his answer.

"I'm not the one who needs coffee, Lo." He uses my nickname without me having to tell him and I want to fucking kiss this man. I wonder if he has had any women take charge before or if he is the one who is always in the driver's seat. With his star status, I am guessing he likes to wait for the clear 'go ahead' sign before he makes his move, but with the intensity of the last hours, he must know he has the 'go ahead' from me. Right? The server brings out my black coffee and our waters, leaving a pitcher for us to refill our glasses if we need.

"I only need coffee to make sure I don't fall asleep on the way back to the condo," I tell him. "I am rather sober, considering the excitement of the last hour of this date."

Instead of agreeing, he says, "Let's take this into the other room. There are couches, and you can have your coffee there." He grabs the pitcher of water and one of the glasses while I take my coffee mug and follow him into what must be a sitting room with a big couch. The couch is not historically correct, so I guess they brought this in for this date since he rented the house for us.

We place our items on the table in front of us. I flop down into the soft couch cushions and put my legs up on the table, ankles crossed. I don't want to flash him with my mini skirt on… or maybe I do. Ezra's eyes follow from my heels up to my legs and to my face. While making eye contact, I use my hand to pat the couch for him to sit right next to me. He sits beside me, and I can feel the lighting strike with our bodies this close. Sex with this man is going to be fireworks, standing ovation type of sex.

I lay my head back on the couch close to his shoulder, placing my hand on his stomach and slightly pulling at his shirt to bring his eyes directly to mine. I lick my lips, so he knows the invitation is there, and his eyes are locked on mine until they shift to watch my tongue wet my lips. He leans in closer, but before our lips touch, he says in a whisper, "London, I'm going to kiss you."

I nod yes, and my eyes are watching his mouth when I whisper back, "Ezra, I really want you to kiss me."

That comment is all it takes because he licks his lips, and our lips connect. First, it is a soft kiss, testing to see if this chemistry is real, but then he places his hand on my thigh, and I immediately feel that tingle between my legs. I move my hand up his chest and open my lips for him. With my invitation, he deepens the kiss, and our tongues dance together in a seductive lip lock. This kiss is so powerful, sexy, and all-consuming that I don't think I will ever be able to enjoy kissing another man. I think he knows it too, because I moan in his mouth and when he turns my legs to drape across his lap, I can feel exactly the effect my kiss is having. I am cheering in my head because Ezra has the biggest dick, and I am a bit nervous I won't be able to handle all of it. But London Isle is no quitter, and I will be damned if I don't manage it.

When I feel how excited he is I am in the zone. All I want to do is feel that cock push up against me. I pull on his shoulder, so we go backward on the couch, and he climbs on top of me. I open my legs to give him space, knowing this skirt will not stay in place because, let's face it, I am absolutely not wearing panties, and we are making out like teenagers whose parents are not home.

I am pulling him closer when he breaks the kiss to look down at me. He sees that my skirt has come up, despite how hard I was trying to keep it in place, and he runs his fingers down my naked pussy. He says against my lips, "I told you, no panties."

I bite his lip and say, "You must have x-ray vision."

He rocks his hard cock into me, and I squeeze his tight ass as he rocks three more times. Between the kissing he is saying, "I will not come in my pants, London."

I am smiling into our kiss when I mumble, "Is that something you would not be proud of, Everest?"

"Fuck no, I wouldn't be proud. I have more control than that. But you are making me lose all control." Just as he says that he slips one finger, then a second, in my pussy and we both inhale sharply with our lips touching.

"Fuck, you are so wet," he states before pumping his fingers slowly.

"Yes, I have been fucking wet for you the last hour of this date."

"You should have told me. I could have helped you," he says with another slow pump of his fingers and his lips on my neck. He is moving slowly on purpose to tease me because he knows I need more pressure and speed. "Do my fingers feel like you imagined they would?"

"Fuck, Ezra, better, please more. I want to come."

"But what about that vibrator? I thought it got your orgasm tonight."

I kiss him deeply and when I come up for air, I moan, "You can have it if you give me more."

He removes his fingers from my pussy and then runs them up to clit to make three very slow circles.

"Everest, you are being a tease." I am pleading with my eyes for him to give me more. He rocks his hard dick into me again, and I officially think dry humping is my new favorite thing.

He says, "I'm not teasing, London, only taking a small taste," and I watch him take his fingers off my clit and put them in his mouth. "You taste amazing."

I moan at his comment and wrap my arms around his neck to pull him back down for another all-consuming tongue kiss. He rocks his hips against me again and says, "Damn, my dick is so fucking hard."

I reach down to stroke him through his jeans and say, "You are so fucking big."

He attacks my mouth with his kisses again and I try to pull his hips back to me. "Fuck, we should stop," he says while still devouring my mouth.

I breathe, "We totally should."

Kiss, rock. "It's the first date and I didn't bring any condoms."

Kiss, rock. I add, "Then we can't do this, for sure." I deepened the kiss and stroked him again.

"Fuck, London. I want you."

"I want you to. Let me help you come. No penetration required."

"Fuck, that sounds so goddamn hot coming out of your mouth."

Kiss. Rock. I moan as he keeps rocking, but I don't want to come like this. I tell him, "Ezra, I will come if you keep rocking against my clit like that."

"I know, I want to see you come."

"Wait, no, I can come watching you explode in my hand. I want to touch you."

I unbuckle his pants and stick my hand in to pull him free and wrap my hands around his huge dick. I push on his shoulder so that he sits back, and I lift myself to a sitting position beside him with his cock in my hand. I begin to stroke him slowly at first, allowing the pressure in my grip to build, and when his head falls back on the couch and he says, "Yes, fuck, like that, London," I know I have him in the spot I want him.

I lean in to kiss his shoulder and whisper in his ear, "Look at me while I have my hands on your dick, Ezra." His eyes snap to mine. I lick his lips and his neck and then go back to fucking his mouth with my tongue. He has his hand on my ass and moves his fingers to my pussy, putting two fingers inside.

"Are you wetter?" he asks.

"Yes."

"Shit, I am so close."

I order, "Look at me when you come, Everest, my eyes, my hands." I kiss him deeply. "My mouth is what you want."

"Yes, fuck," he hisses as I increase my speed. He hooks his fingers and does the 'come here motion' that sends me over the edge. But I twist and add just enough pressure to ensure that he is coming with me by the time I am whisper-shouting his name to keep the staff from hearing us.

Our eyes are still locked when he kisses me with that all-consuming mouth of his. He slows the kiss enough to say, "Next time you will come on my face and my dick."

"I just like the idea of there being a next time," I say honestly as he brings his fingers back around to his mouth to taste me again. I help him put his semi-hard cock back in his pants, and I can't stop myself from saying, "I had a great first date with you, Ezra Everest."

He smiles at me using his whole name. "This has been the best first date I have had in years, London Isle."

The need to kiss him again is so intense. We keep kissing for what seems like forever until we both come up for air.

Reluctantly, I say, "I should go. Amelia and I have so much to do tomorrow for this project and I need to hire a new project manager."

I reached down to check his watch to see the time because neither of us has our phones. I kiss his lips again and slowly crawl off his lap, stand up, fix my skirt, and put my boobs back in my shirt, because the second make-out session was getting much hotter, and without a condom, we couldn't finish what I wanted to finish. Well, we could, I have an IUD for birth control, but I would not want to pressure him or make him feel uncomfortable about using no protection with a woman he just met, especially because of his star status. I don't want him to have negative thoughts about my intentions; not that I think he would, but I wouldn't blame him if he did. There are women in the world who would do those things to men like him.

"We have the house for the whole night. You could stay, and we could just sleep," he says with knowing in his eyes.

I state matter-of-factly, "I would not be able to sleep with you, knowing how much I want to feel you in me. You don't have condoms and I don't have the willpower to resist. I should go."

He has joy in his expression when he laughs, saying, "I'm glad to know that I destroy your willpower that much."

"Yes. Yes, you do."

He walks me to the door, where we find my clutch and keys by the entryway. Ezra hands me his cell phone and asks, "Can I have your number?"

I can't stop the excitement that builds in me. "You can have my number." I try to play it cool, but he sees straight through my demeanor.

He walks me out to my SUV, which is nicely parked right in front of the door. We kiss for another what feels like fifteen minutes, and I can feel his hard cock against my stomach again. I unlock the car, and he opens the door for me. We kiss some more before I finally pull away and say goodnight.

He closes the door and I give him one last wave before driving away. I get to the end of the road before I let out a scream of pure excitement and touch my lips as I make the drive back to my condo. Ezra Everest likes me, and I hope with all the good karma I deserve that he will call me.

Chapter Four

I still can't wipe the smile off my face when I make it to the condo. I am so happy after this date. Not only was the physical chemistry there but we are on the same level mentally. The communication was of a higher caliber and we both have big life goals. I am still floating as I enter the condo; I cannot stop thinking about him, his lips, his hands, his words.

While I am removing my makeup and getting ready for bed, Ami scares me when she sticks her head into the bathroom and says, "Details now." She closes the lid on the toilet and sits there waiting.

I am not going to tell her everything, but I do want to tell her some things. "Oh my gosh, Amelia, I had the best time ever. I thought he was going to be fake and surface level, you know, all 'I'm a movie star so you will like me.' But he showed me some of who he really is, not just the famous person. We talked about everything."

Ami jumps in. "Like what? Details."

"We talked about my company, his climb to fame, his family—because you know my family is a dark hole—religion, politics, sex, all the social movements, business goals, life goals … it was so much that I'm not sure we will have anything to talk about when we see each other again."

"Wait, you made plans to see each other again?" Ami asks excitedly.

"Not official plans, but he asked for my number, and I gave it to him. Like my real number, not your number to have my call screened."

Amelia jumps up and squeals. "Ahhhh, I am so proud of me, I made you a real connection!"

I laugh at her doing her happy dance, even though she is trying to take credit for this evening. "Ami, I will give you credit for setting the date, but the connection I felt tonight, that was all me and him. God, I hope he calls. I know he is here for some big meeting, reading scripts, and working on some secret project. I really hope he puts in the effort to make time for me."

Amelia hugs me from behind with her excitement and looks at me in the mirror. "He will call. It sounds like you both had a great night, and he got to be himself, not the version he lets the public have."

"We really did. And the kissing. Oh my, Ami … I cannot even put into words how hot and perfect the kissing was."

She is squeezing me so tight. "Why didn't you lead with the fact that you kissed him, London? That is so hot!"

"Ami, I can't breathe, and you're screaming in my ear." She lets go of me to do her dance as she walks out the bathroom door. I follow her.

"You know I don't kiss and tell. That's all you'll get. Know that the chemistry and connection were there. I'm so glad we make poor decisions when we drink red wine. I think this poor decision is going to give me some true happiness, even if it's only temporary."

Ami hugs me again and says, "Don't count him out; maybe he is looking for the same commitment you're looking for and you guys can make it work. We have airplanes so distance is not an issue, and I can schedule secret meetings for you two when your schedules allow. Not to sound cliché, but if you guys want it to work and it is meant to be, it will be."

I nod my head in agreement. "I'll just live in the moment and see where it takes us. But God, do I hope…" I don't even finish that sentence because it is filled with too many unanswered questions and so much optimism. I just tell Ami goodnight and let her know that we need to start our day tomorrow by 7 a.m.

* * * *

By noon, my previous high from the date is wearing off because there are so many issues coming at me with the contractors for this project. Without a project manager, the contractors seem to be completely lost. It does not make sense to me. I am ready to fire them all, but then I get a delivery of the most stunning flower arrangement. The flowers are all unique and a few of them are unfamiliar to me. Ami is dancing around the vase and clapping her hands while I read the card in private.

Challenge accepted. I am trying to get all your EFFORT.
--Ez

I have a teenager's first crush smile when I look back at Ami to say, "We have our own coded language."

I want to scream and do my own happy dance, but I can't because when I look up, the owner of the construction company I've hired is standing at the door of the co-working office. Before he can even complain, I raise my hand. "Peter, I know, I'm working on getting another project manager. Just follow the plans and keep working on the things you can complete now."

He takes a deep breath. "Ms. Isle," he says. I have told him so many times to call me London, but he will not listen. "I'm not here for that. I have a recommendation for the project manager position. I wanted to give you her name in person and ask you to give her a shot."

"Tell us who it is, and Ami will set the interview. I am open to recommendations, especially if it will keep this project on the timeline we have all agreed to."

Peter gives me a long-drawn-out story about his recommendation getting pregnant in high school and being a single mom but having worked her way through college and now having her master's in human resources but her undergraduate degree in construction management.

I stopped him. "Peter, you don't have to sell me the person; just tell me her name, and I will meet with her."

He exhales and says, "The thing is, it's my grandson's mother. My asshole of a son ran off on her, but I've made sure to be a pawpaw to my grandson and to help where I can when she allows it. I just think Elle, I mean Ellen, would work perfectly with you and Amelia."

I simply smile at Peter. I can tell he is unsure of my reaction to this recommendation, but he shouldn't be. I am a firm believer that you should work your ass off and use every avenue you legally can to get the things you want. The avenue needs to be something you can live with, but you have to know that you gave it your all to accomplish your goal.

"Tell her to come in tomorrow at," Ami jumps in, "10:30 a.m."

I continue, "10:30 a.m. for the interview. Call her and have her email over her resume and three professional references."

"Thank you, Ms. Isle."

Before he can leave, I add, "Peter, you really should call me London. I'll just keep reminding you. It will make me feel so much better."

He just smiles and shakes his head no before leaving the office, and I go back to enjoying my flowers.

* * * *

It's after 5 p.m. before I can come up for air and take a break from this project. Ami left a few hours ago because she has permits and other tasks to accomplish while we're here. My phone ringing breaks my concentration and I think it is likely Ami, but when I look at the caller ID, I don't recognize the number. Accepting the call, I don't even think that it could be Ezra until I hear his smooth voice on the line.

"London Isle," I say in the way of hello.

"Hello, London Isle, this is Ezra Everest. I had my lips on you last night."

I lean back in my chair to enjoy this call and the smile in my voice is undeniable. "Oh yeah. Really? Not sure that that sounds like something I would do. I do have a vague recollection of an amazing date with an Ezra, though," I say with sarcasm, listening to him laugh before I continue. "Thank you for my amazingly thoughtful and beautiful flowers. You're setting a precedent. I hope you can hold out?"

"Oh, I'm so glad you like them. I do love a good challenge, London. Did you read the card?"

"I did, and it made me smile for hours."

"Good answer, London."

"True answer, Ezra."

"My assistant told me it was boring and that you wouldn't understand. I had to threaten to fire her if she changed the message."

I laugh. "I told Ami that we officially have our own secret language. She thought I was crazy but couldn't stop her MC Hammer dance at the thought of you sending me, and I quote, 'the good kind of flowers for your flower snob-ish ass.'"

I can tell that he is also smiling when he says, "She sounds delightful."

"She really is. Hiring her was one of the best decisions of my professional and personal life. But don't tell her I said that, or she'll want another raise."

He keeps talking and I can hear cars outside; he must be traveling. "Were you able to get the project under control with the contractors and find a new manager?"

I love that he is asking about the crisis I told him about yesterday. "I was able to get the contractors back on track. Ami set me up four manager interviews for tomorrow, and one came recommended by the construction company owner I'm working with. I'm looking forward to meeting her; she seems like a good match for me and Ami."

"That's good news, honey."

"Wow, 'honey,' did that just slip out or are you with someone you don't want to know my name?" I am curious about his answer.

He makes a point to say, "London, that just came out. I can say your name anywhere, honey."

"Oh good, because I like to hear you say my name." We laugh at the reference to the song and the sexual tone of the joke.

"I want to see you tonight; are you free?" he asks.

That's the one sentence I had hoped he would say to me on this call. "Yes. I want to see you too. I can come to you." I check the clock before asking, "What time are you thinking?"

"I can come to you because I'm already out. It will be easier to come out to where you are and there'll be fewer people to see me. I can bring dinner?"

"I will make the drinks and dessert. If you're interested in dessert."

"London, I am very interested in your dessert," he states matter-of-factly. "Let's say 8 p.m. tonight. Does the condo you're in have a private entrance?"

"If you pull into the parking garage, I can buzz you in and then you can enter through the garage elevator, so you don't have to worry about being seen."

"Thank you, London. I know this may seem like I'm treating you like a secret. I just don't like my personal life exposed to the public until I'm ready, and until you're ready. People get too obsessed with celebrities sometimes, and I don't want any stalkers or crazy fans speculating about us."

"Ezra, you don't have to explain; I know your star status, and I'm not ready for any cameras in my face, my business, or my family backstory. We can take this as slow as you like."

He exhales heavily. "I don't know where you have been my whole life, but I'm thanking the Creator right now for placing you in my path. Honey, I'll see you at eight. Okay. Bye."

He's gone before I can say anything, but I do know that I can't have Ami at the condo tonight. I booked her a room at Hotel Bennett in Charleston's historic district and then email her the confirmation. This means I get an immediate call from her.

"OMG, are you seeing him again tonight and kicking me out of the condo?" she asks.

"Yes. That's exactly what's happening. I got you a suite and you can have dinner on me."

"You know I love when you spoil me. What time is he going to be there so I can be out of the place?"

"8 p.m."

"Okay. I'm headed to get some clothes and I will see you at the office in the morning. The first interview is at 9 a.m."

"Thanks, Amelia. Oh, will you pick up some IPAs and local beer for the condo? I'm in charge of drinks and dessert. You know I suck at wines, and I really want beer tonight."

"Yes. I know the perfect place to pick up good beers and it's on my way to the condo. For dessert, I'm sure he wants you, but I'll stop at the cupcake truck to get a few for the place. I got it. You get home and make the space ready for y'all's dinner. If that's what you want to call it."

"You are the worst."

"You love me," Ami says as a way to end the call.

I wrap up my work and get back to the condo with only an hour to get ready. Ami has already set everything up nicely, made sure the condo was presentable, and even put a big box of condoms on my bed. I laughed at her intuitiveness because I was thinking when I got in the elevator that I should have gotten condoms. Before I jump in the shower, I text Ezra the address, gate code, door code, and condo number, so he can come straight up without having to wait for me to let him in. I don't want him to feel ambushed by any of the people in the building. I take a fast shower, reapply my makeup, and put on skin-tight skinny jeans that I have to jump to get into and a sexy black one-shoulder shirt. My hair is half up, and I've decided to go without shoes since I'm in my temporary home. It's a corporate rental, so there's nothing too exciting about the place, but it's in a great location and it's safe. It comes with a nice kitchen, big bathtubs, and plenty of room for me and Ami. It isn't personalized, like my home, but that just gives me something to look forward to showing Ezra one day.

There is a knock at the door, and I'm glad he didn't have any trouble using the codes to get into the building. I open it to see the sexiest man alive—I'm pretty sure that is literal based on magazine covers—at my door wearing a baseball t-shirt, a baseball cap pulled low, and jeans that ride his hips just low enough that if he lifted his arms, I would see that gorgeous 'V' muscle that leads to that marvelous thick cock of his. He is drinking me in too when I grab his arm and pull him inside for a big hug.

"Hey Ezra," I say as I pull back from the perfect greeting hug.

But that is not enough for him, because he places his lips on mine and kisses me like a starving man. My toes curl from the intensity of the embrace and when the kiss finale slows, he stays close to my lips as he murmurs, "Hey London."

He's holding what smells like Chinese takeout, so I lead him to the kitchen where I pull out plates, silverware, and glasses out for us. We're talking about his day when I set an IPA on the table for him and he pulls me into his lap to kiss me again.

"I get that kind of treatment for beer?" I ask. "That's so sexy, Everest." I get up to get myself a locally brewed beer because I am not a fan of IPAs, but he kisses my hip over my shirt and squeezes my ass before I can pull away to get my drink.

I hope he can see the lust in my eyes. "You're very into physical touch tonight. Is that a normal thing you do after finger fucking a girl?"

He coughs. I've caught him off guard with my comment and he's nearly choking on his drink. "The things you say. You should see the normal things I'll do after I eat your pussy tonight." That sets fire to my bones and stops me mid-sip.

He doesn't take his eyes off me as he continues, "Let's eat, London. You'll need your strength."

"Promises, promises. I do hope you can deliver," I tease, but there's no hiding how excited I am. Dinner goes quickly and is filled with talk of the day, sexual references, touches, and kisses. It seems like a date that people who have been in a relationship for years would have, not people who met yesterday. Everything seems so easy and right now all I want to do is fuck. I am all about consensual sexual freedom. I don't believe in being shy about what I want in the bedroom, and I think everyone can have their own kinks. As long as the two parties participating consent, then I say go for it. You only live once and everyone should experience sex that gives them multiple orgasms. Saying all that, I know that it takes work and trust to build a true sexual connection with your partner where you feel safe enough to tell them what truly turns you on. I can imagine Ezra has had every type of sex, but I want sex with me to be an experience he will never want to finish, leave, or forget. So, I've decided that I'm not going to pretend with him. Instead, I'll let him say when he has had enough.

We have been on the couch touching, kissing, listening to music through the speakers, and talking, just connecting on all levels, when I ask him, "Do you like it when women are commanding or when they ask for what they want in bed?"

I want to know the answer before we take it past the touching. He says, "I think that in order for either of us to be pleased sexually you need to know what your partner wants, so you have to tell me. Especially since I can't read minds." He laughs and kisses me. "Why? Are you demanding in bed, London? Will it take all my powers to please you?"

"I wouldn't say demanding. I would say that in the past I have had to provide directions, and that has turned men off. Likely causing the end of a few relationships," I tell him with a serious tone to my voice.

"Well, rest assured, I take direction well, but I promise I don't need much guidance. I'm positive I can make you scream for me."

With that comment, I move to straddle him on the couch, adding, "I don't want to think about other women touching you. I only want to think about what you promised me in the kitchen about this sexy-as-sin mouth of yours eating me like your last meal."

With that, I kiss him with abandonment and trust that he will give me what my body desires. He pulls my shirt over my head, and I help him with his. We stare at each other before he slides his arm up my back and opens the clasp on my strapless bra, letting it fall to the couch between us.

He cups my breasts in his hands before taking one in his mouth, where he sucks a nipple and flicks it with his tongue. I run my hands down the curve of his thick and well-defined chest, making my way to the eight-pack of abs that is begging to be licked. He looks at me long enough to see my desire and asks, "Is Ami coming in tonight? Do we need to move to another room?"

I shake my head no as he takes my nipple back in his mouth. "Oooh, that feels good," I moan as he switches nipples and starts sucking. I realize how much I want to see all of him; I didn't get to see everything last night when we were touching and dry humping. I pull my nipple out of his mouth and stand up in front of him.

"I want to see you. Take off your clothes," I say.

He stands and, without taking his eyes off mine, removes his shoes, unbuckles his belt and pants, and lets them fall to the floor. His boxer briefs are tented by his massive dick. When I get ready to touch him, he stops me by removing his briefs and stepping out of them. He's standing before me completely naked for my eyes to take in. When my gaze doesn't travel past his hard cock, he strokes it for me to see. I can't take it anymore. I kiss him like my life depends on his mouth connecting with mine. I run my hands all over his body because I need to feel all of him.

Ezra has other plans, though, because he leans back from my kiss and unzips my jeans. We work together to get the skintight material over my ass and down my hips. He kneels to give more pull, but the jeans don't budge. We're laughing at our struggle when he says, "These are sexy, but they take too long to get off, and London, you're not wearing panties again."

"Oops," I say. He kisses my hip, turns me around, and pushes me back onto the couch. He pulls my jeans the rest of the way off and tosses them somewhere behind us. I look up and find that he is on his knees in front of me licking his lips, not looking at my face but at my center.

Not feeling even slightly shy, I run my fingers over my nipples and down my body while he watches. He watches me touch my clit and slide my fingers into myself. He quickly removes my fingers with his hand and says, "No, I got this."

He starts kissing his way down my body and when he reaches my sex, he places one of my legs over his shoulder and then pushes the other leg wide, which he holds down with his hand. I am completely exposed to him, and I couldn't be more turned on.

"London, when I lick you, are you going to soak my face?"

I moan at his words. "Ezra. Fuck. Yes, I am. I want your tongue so bad."

He asks, as close as he can get to my center without putting his mouth on me, "You want to ride my tongue?"

"Oh yes. Fuck me with your mouth."

He moans at my response and gives me what I want. He licks me from slit to clit, and we both moan at the connection. He has me moaning and wanting to come within minutes. I put my hands in his hair and tell him, "I need you to suck on my clit and put your fingers in me. I am so close; let me come."

Not to be rushed, Ezra fucks me with his tongue, and I am panting by the time he slips two fingers in me and sucks my clit into his mouth. I come apart all over his face and he laps up all my juices. I am shouting, "Fuck yes, right there, Ezra," when he sticks his tongue back in me. I push him away and try to close my legs because I can't take any more of his mouth after coming so hard, but he holds my legs open and says, "We're just getting started, London."

He reaches under his discarded pants on the floor, and I watch him roll a condom down his thick head and length. His eyes meet mine as he says, "I want to fuck you with my rock-hard cock."

This man and his dirty talk do things to me. "Yes, I want more," is all I can get my mouth to say before he is hovering over me on the couch. I threw one leg over the back of the couch to make room for him to get between my legs and I put the other around his waist. I reach my hand down to his shaft and guide him to my entrance. It has been more than a year since I've had sex, but right now all I can think about is how much I want him.

Ezra enters me slowly and presses his forehead to mine when he is less than half inside me. "Honey, I need you to relax and let me in."

"Damn, that isn't all of you? I feel so full."

He kisses me deeply and I inhale, ready for more. He continues to kiss me, taking my mind off his entrance into me, until I feel him brushing what feels like my cervix. "Fuck Ezra, yes, I can take all of you."

He leans in my ear and bites my shoulder. "You are so fucking tight and feel so good. I'm going to move now." And with that warning, we move in rhythm as he pumps into me.

I watch as his abs and hip muscles work to bring us to climax. I am kissing his chest, neck, and mouth, moaning and clawing at his back, trying to get him closer and deeper in me than is likely possible. Our rhythm is so perfect.

I angle my hips slightly differently and meet his thrusts as he says, "London, fuck, babe, I'm going to come. I want to feel you come on my cock."

He pinches my clit and nipple with the perfect amount of pressure and pain, and I come so hard on his dick that it is like a vise wrapping around him. "Oh wow, fuck, Ezra, right there. I'm coming."

With a moan, our eyes connect. "Fuck, London, yes," he says and fills the condom with his seed.

With him still inside me, we both take a moment to bring our breathing back down. That was intense and the eye contact made the orgasm so much stronger; I usually can't come in this position and never while looking into someone's eyes. But the push on my clit while he was pumping and how deep he was … it was the perfect force to satisfy me. I realize how quickly I'm becoming attached to him.

I rub his back while we adjust to that mind-blowing orgasm and say, "Wow."

He adds, "I don't think 'wow' covers it," as he pulls out of me. He sits back to pull off the condom and tie it off.

"The bathroom is in my bedroom, first door on the right," I tell him.

He gets up and I follow him to the bedroom. I throw back the covers on the bed to get in while he cleans up in the bathroom. I hear the toilet flush and water running before he comes to lie beside me on the bed. I rub my hands up his body and we are lying in comfortable silence when his touches move lower, playing with my slit.

With lust in his voice and his mouth on my nipple, he asks, "Did I hurt you, London?"

"Not any more than I wanted you to hurt me. It had been a while since I had sex. I thought I'd need more recovery time. I don't. Did you need more? Was there something different you wanted me to do?"

"Honey, you were epic. So tight and wet for me. I only wished there was nothing between us. I want to feel all of you." I understand what he is saying, but before I can respond, he whispers into my chest while kissing my body, "This may be too much, but I'm saying it because I don't want any misunderstandings. We were really connected and in sync. I have never felt that before during sex. I don't think I have ever come so hard."

He is still playing with my slit and kissing my body when I tell him, "Well, babe, you haven't seen anything yet. Wait until I make you come with my mouth. You'll see stars when I finish giving you a blow job."

"London, such promises. Can you really deliver? I want to see stars." He jokes. I can see the humor in his eyes.

"Just you wait; you will never want another woman's mouth on your cock once you've had mine."

"I believe you because I've already had enough of you to know that I don't want anyone else." With that comment, I roll him onto his back and kiss him passionately until I can feel his dick get hard again for me.

"Can you go again, Everest?" I ask with humor in my tone because I already know he can.

"I do believe you can feel the answer to that question. I left the condoms in the other room."

"I have some in the drawer." I reach above him, and my breasts are in his face. He takes the opportunity to suck one into his mouth and proceeds to give my breast hickies.

"Are we teenagers now? Hickies? Are you marking me?" I asked him, breathless from his mouth on me.

"Do I need to mark you, London?"

"No, it's just you."

"I like that answer, London. Put the condom on."

I roll it down his shaft and then lower myself onto him. We both sigh when I am seated on him, taking so much of him, and with his hands on my ass, he helps me ride him until we are both moaning and breathing heavily. He sits up and we are nose to nose as I keep going, moving so close to my climax. We are watching where our bodies connect and the sex is getting faster when I say, "Ezra, I am so full of your cock."

That has him biting my lip and then flipping me over to put my ass in the air. "I am going to feel you come on my dick while I fuck you from behind. Hold on, baby, this won't be gentle."

He's right, it isn't gentle, but it is fucking perfect, so perfect that when I come, I dig my nails into his hip and ass, likely leaving marks. And when my nails dig in, he grabs my hair and pulls me up so he can kiss me as he comes into that barrier between us. We collapse as a tangle of bodies on my bed and take a moment to catch our breath.

"Damn, London," he nearly shouts, stretching out the pronunciation of my name.

"I know. I'm pretty sure I saw fireworks behind my eyes at the end."

He rolls off me and pulls me around to face him.

I asked him, "Are you okay? Was that too much? I think I probably bruised your hip with my nails."

"I don't care; your ass while I was pounding you from behind will be forever in my memory."

"Good, because the look in your eyes when we were face-to-face isn't something I will ever forget either."

He kisses me softly and we make out for a while before he gets up to throw away the condom again. I use the bathroom and then check the clock. I have an early day tomorrow, but I really hope he is spending the night. Shower sex in the morning is on my to-do list.

"Will you stay the night?" I ask uncertainly when I get back into the bed with him.

"Yes, if that's okay with you?" he asks, making sure I know I have the option to send him home.

"Yes, I want you to stay. Shower sex sounds like a morning activity I want to do with you."

He kisses my nose and then my mouth again. We must both be tired after all that work we just put in because it takes us no time to fall asleep together, entwined in one another and face-to-face.

Chapter Five

Ezra and I spend all of our free time together while we are both in South Carolina. He comes to my rental every evening he's free and when he can't make it, we talk on FaceTime for hours. I give him the condo door code so that he can come to my place if it's late and crawl into bed with me.

The first time I come back to the rental and he's there on the couch surrounded by work and on a conference call, I am immediately turned on. Something about coming home to find my man—yes, I said my man—relaxed and building his success sends me into overdrive.

Stalking over to the couch, I stand in front of him while he talks about contracts and scheduling. I look down at him while he works, just watching, and my body heats up like a furnace. He looks up at me and smiles, giving me the 'Why do you look like that?' stare. He puts his phone on mute while the other people on the call are discussing or arguing about something, I can't tell because all I can think is, Ezra was here waiting for me to get home. It gives me so many butterflies because I now think this relationship is moving on the path that says, 'Let's go the distance.'

"Babe, why do you look like that? What's wrong?" he asks while the others are talking.

"Do you know how sexy I find it that you are on this couch working on your empire and waiting for me to get home?" I say as I kneel in front of him and place my hands on his knees.

"Oh really, that does it for you?" Ezra says. He watches me run my hands up his strong, thick thighs.

"Yes, it really does. I'm about to show you just what it does for me." He raises his hips to help me pull his joggers down his legs, and I lick his hard shaft from root to tip.

"You think you can focus on that call while I blow you?" I ask, taking his cock in my mouth. His eyes connect with mine.

"I'm not sure," he says with a long moan as I suck the tip of his cock and use my hands to pump him.

In the background, I hear someone say, "Ezra, what do you think?"

He unmutes his phone and says, "Um," and draws in a long breath, still watching me as I keep sucking him. "Um, Jesus, yes. I mean no. Guys, give me thirty minutes. I'll call you back."

He hangs up the phone just as a string of fucks come out of his mouth. I work my mouth and hands all over his cock until he is warning me that he is going to come. I relax my throat so that I can take him deep without gagging. My gag reflex is not very sensitive, which allows me to take his huge cock very deep. His hand is on the back of my head and running through my hair while I show him what my skills can do.

"Oh God, London. Yes. Yes. All of me. No hands, babe. Take all of him." He is talking about his cock as if it is another person, and he is clearly enjoying this. I double my efforts, take away my hands, and then his hot seed hits the back of my throat. I swallowed it all.

As he catches his breath, he says, "Oh baby, I didn't even know I needed that. Your mouth is magic."

"I'm glad you approve." I moved up the couch to sit next to him. He tries to help me out of my clothes, but I tell him to finish his call first and then finish me later. With a hard and passionate kiss, he does, and then makes sure I see stars three times before we go to sleep.

* * * *

We develop a comfortable routine while we finish our stay in South Carolina. I'm sad to leave because I don't know how we are going to do long distance. Ami has told me not to stress over it because she and V, Ezra's assistant, will work out the schedule. I'm still worried, though, because it's a new relationship and I really want it to work.

During our last dinner in Charleston, I am in a quiet mood. He doesn't push me to express myself while we're at the restaurant. But when we get back to the rental, I can tell he has had enough of my standoffish attitude.

"London, what's wrong? You've been quiet all night. You barely touched your food."

"I'm trying not to complain or be difficult. So, I'm just keeping my comments to myself," I tell him as I walk to the kitchen, passing him, to place my leftovers in the fridge.

"What does that mean?" he asks as he follows me. "Don't walk away when we're talking." He seems annoyed that I would brush past him while he is clearly trying to have a serious conversation with me.

We're standing in the kitchen with the table between us. I voice my concerns to him. "Ezra, I'm leaving to go back to North Carolina tomorrow and then I'll be in Nebraska for like ten months on and off. I don't even know where you're going next. It makes me sad to think this may be over before it even gets started."

He crosses the kitchen to stand directly in front of me. "Honey, this is not over. We are just getting started, like you said. I'm in and invested in this and there is no way I can stop this before I see where it goes. I know you will be in North Carolina and Nebraska. I'll make sure that we see each other every month and talk with each other every day. This will not end over distance." He kisses my lips to reassure me.

"Are you sure? I know who you are and how busy you can be. I don't want us making promises and breaking them. I'm scared to get my hopes up." I keep giving him my truth because he needs to know. "I really like you. I want to keep seeing you and see how we grow together, but I don't want to sidetrack your goals or life plans."

"My goals and life plans adjust as things change in my life. Babe, I assure you that this, us, is something I want too. I really like you, London. I am willing to put in the work to build this, even if it means flying back and forth to Nebraska or North Carolina to see you."

It isn't lost on me that he said 'us.' His words fill my heart with so much hope because he wants to try and make this relationship work. I'm so excited that I hug and kiss him before saying, "Yes, me too. I will put in whatever effort we need to see where this goes."

"Let's start with me coming to North Carolina in a few days," he says with a smile, surprising me with this news.

"Really? That would be awesome. You can see my place and I can show you my town." I'm already planning in my head all the things I want to do.

"Yes, really. I know you're leaving tomorrow. I'm wrapping up here so instead of going to LA right away, I'll spend a few days with you in North Carolina. I already have a flight booked. I'll be there at the end of the week and stay through the following week."

I kiss his mouth as he tries to tell me his plans. He smiles at my excitement. I can't believe he has already started changing his schedule to fit me into his life. I am so moved by this. He is making space for me in his life, and I love it.

He keeps explaining, "I can do video business meetings and read scripts from anywhere, so North Carolina is where I'm choosing to do those things."

"That makes me so happy, Ezra. I can't wait to show you all the things I've done with my small town, and you can see me in my environment." I'm nervous and excited to show him all that is North Carolina and I want to show him all my plans for Nebraska too. I want him to be proud of me and to see the success that I have amassed in my corner of the world.

Chapter Six

The rest of the week goes by so slowly, and it seems like it takes Ezra's arrival day forever to get here. But he is true to his word; we talk every night when I get back to NC and text a few times throughout the day.

I'm so excited to see him and pick him up from the airport. I've never been in the private arrival section of Raleigh/Durham International Airport, but there is such a section, and I'm waiting patiently for Ezra to arrive. I'm not sure if I'm supposed to play it cool or if I can run up and jump on him when I see him. I am leaning toward running and jumping. I mean, no one is in the arrival section except me and a few staff.

My decision was made for me when I saw Ezra saying goodbye to the flight crew and signing an autograph. So, I wait until he is finished before I approach him, but the intensity in his gaze as he watches me while signing the autograph says exactly how much he can't wait to touch me. He is giving his final handshakes, only slightly breaking eye contact with me to do so, when we both start walking toward each other. Our eyes are locked, and it feels like it takes forever to meet in the middle, but we both take long strides toward each other. Never have I been more appreciative of my long legs than I am at this moment.

I stopped one step away from him because I don't know what the protocol is, and the flight staff are still watching him. He takes the last step into my space but doesn't touch me. He says, "I fucking missed you and I want to kiss you so bad, but my guess is that the staff are watching and still taking photos or videos. I don't want our kisses on the internet. They're just for us. For now."

I want nothing more than to devour his mouth, but he's right. So, I must be content with the sexy eyes he is giving me while we stand in front of one another.

"I fucking missed you too," I say. "Let's go so I can greet you properly."

We make our way to my blacked-out silver Audi Q8. I open the trunk so he can place his luggage inside. The moment the doors are closed, the sexual tension increases by one hundred and our lips connect. This is a kiss that is meant for a movie screen: it is hot, all tongue, and goes on forever. It's like we have never kissed each other before, or like we have both been fasting and can finally have this perfect meal. This kiss touches my soul and makes my heart fall a little further for this beautiful, considerate, and passionate man.

When we finally slow the kiss, he says, "Hey honey."

"Hi baby," is all I can say while we keep our lips together for small kisses and I place my hand on his cheek.

"You know, I'll expect a greeting like this every time we're apart for more than three days. You have officially set a standard," I tell him before I turn the car on.

"I can handle that expectation." He turns my face back to his for more kisses before I put the car in gear, and we are off.

* * * *

We have the perfect week together. I show Ezra my work and my town, and he meets Ami. He has meetings and gets through several scripts. We have mind-blowing sex nightly and it feels like I'm living in a dream. On our last night with each other, we decided to do nothing but be together. We're going to cook, eat dinner, and have sex until neither of us can walk.

We need food to start off our night, and that means a grocery store trip. Ezra drives me to the store but doesn't get out because he doesn't want to be recognized in the store. We've had a good week; he's only been recognized and approached five times. I am betting five times is considered nothing, or at least very minimal, to him. So, he lets me out at the door and goes to park while I am inside.

On my way back to the car, I see James, walking right towards me with a shit-eating grin on his face. Fuck. This is not going to be good. I can't tell if Ezra can see what is about to happen. James is a fuckboy that I'd had sex with from time to time when I was drunk or stressed. I don't like James at all, but he has a big cock and eats pussy like it is his full-time job. After we work out my stress by fucking, he leaves, and I never return any of his calls until the next time I need a decent lay. But James always thinks when he sees me that he is supposed to go home with me and fuck. I hope this doesn't go badly. I keep walking and pretend not to see him.

But he says, "The fuck, London. You're going to act like you don't see me?"

I have to play it off. "Oh, James, I'm sorry. I was in my own world. Hey. Hope you are well."

I don't lean in to hug him, thinking he won't lean in if I don't, but I am not that lucky. He scoops me into a big hug, lifts me off my feet, and grabs my ass all at the same time. He is sliding me back down his body when he leans into my ear to say, "You look so good. I can come by after I finish in the store."

I pat his shoulder and take a big step back before saying, "No. I'm good. Busy."

But James is not one to back down from something he wants. He steps back into my space and says, "Come on, London. My dick is hard already just thinking about your tits bouncing while you ride me."

I can feel Ezra's arrival before I see him. I should have known it would be too much to ask for him to be on a call or checking an email and missing this interaction. Ezra puts his hand on my shoulder and pulls me out of James's space and then places a possessive hand in my back pocket, right on my ass. James seems shocked that someone removed me from his space.

I place a hand on Ezra's chest and say, "Ezra, this is a friend of mine, James. James, this is Ezra."

James gives him a once over and there is no recognition on his face. He hasn't connected the dots on who Ezra is, and I hope it stays that way.

Ezra says, "James, it's nice to meet you, but you're standing too close and touching too much of my girlfriend."

James looks shocked and says, "Yeah, right. London doesn't do relationships, buddy. Don't get too attached."

I'm shocked and offended by James's deduction of me. I just don't do relationships with James. He is an asshole and so full of himself. He is one of those guys who if you tell him a story, he always has to 'one up' you.

Ezra releases a deep breath. "I assure you that she does and that whatever chance you thought you had, you no longer have it. Don't touch her so intimately again. Let's go, London." He says that last part with no room for compromise; he wants to leave now.

He grabs my hand and the cart to leave, but James isn't finished. "London, call me when you get rid of the Captain America wannabe. I'll remind you what a real man feels like."

Before Ezra says something stupid, I just turn to James and say, "James, always the douche in every conversation." He laughs, but I'm not joking.

I push Ezra along to the car and I can see the anger setting on his shoulders, but he doesn't say anything until we are in the car and all the groceries have been loaded. Before he can explode, I say, "Wait, don't be mad. He was someone I would hook up with when I was drunk or crazy horny. It never meant anything, and he knows that. I don't like him, and he knows that too. He means nothing to me."

I can hear the anger he is trying to hold back in his voice as he asks, "So, why did he think he could touch you like that in public, London? That's how rumors get started in my world and relationships fall apart. He was way too familiar with you."

"He's normally not that touchy. I don't know why he did it today. I'm sorry you had to see that. It wasn't meant to disrespect or embarrass you."

"But you do know how bad that looked? How annoyed I am right now knowing that asshole touched you today or in the past?"

"Ezra, don't be like that. You have past lovers too. Neither of us was a virgin before we met."

"Yes, but I never wanted to see anyone you have been with."

I am shocked by this comment. I don't want to lash out and say something I don't mean but, really, wow. "Really, Ezra Everest, The Mountain? The summit that every woman in the world has asked to climb publicly or privately, Ezra?" I add emphasis to his name. "Will I have that luxury? Will I never meet any woman who has seen you naked? Will I never meet any woman who has held your hand? Let's not let our past relationships get in the way of this relationship. Because if anyone should be jealous, it should be me. I can only imagine all the models, socialites, and movie stars that have felt your lips and your touch. Let's just go before we both say something to ruin the night."

Before pulling away, he looks at me to say, "I didn't like that at all, London. I'm not normally a jealous man. But with you, I am. I don't want other men touching your body that way. This relationship is exclusive. In case you need clarity, there will be no other people in this relationship. Me and you. Agreed." He says it as a statement, not a question for me to consider.

"That means both of us," I say. "If I am exclusive with you then I expect the same respect."

"Yes. I can give you that."

"Are you sure, Ezra? Because there are still a lot of famous, beautiful women in the world. I will not tolerate being made a fool. If you still want to be able to sleep around, now is the time to say that."

"I've done what I wanted enough to know when I have a perfect thing. This is perfect and I will not screw it up by cheating. I promise."

"Okay."

"Okay." We both huff an agreement as he drives back to my home.

We get the groceries in the house but instead of cooking, Ezra pushes me against the table until I am in a seated position. He steps between my legs and then claims my mouth. I lift my hips to help him get my jeans and underwear off and then he eats my pussy like I am his dinner. He doesn't stop until I am screaming his name and begging for more. He stands from the table and pulls my shirt and bra off.

"It's my name you're screaming, London. Your pussy is wet for me. Your nipples are awaiting my mouth," he says as he pinches my nipples just hard enough to cause pleasure and pain.

I moan, "Yes, Ezra. God, it will always be you I want." The words slip out with the fog of orgasm. With that admission, he claims my mouth again and takes off his clothes.

He strokes his cock while I watch and moan. "Everest, no more teasing."

"I want you bare, London. I'm clean. Are you on birth control?"

Oh my gosh. I have wanted to feel just him since before he even got to North Carolina, but I didn't want to pressure him.

"Yes," is all I get out before he enters me. I exhale while he pushes deeper into me. "I have an IUD. I'm clean too."

I moan as he keeps thrusting inside me. He is so deep, and we are both locked in each other's gaze. It is a complete and total claiming. He is all dirty and possessive talk, making sure I know that I am his.

"Do you feel how perfectly our bodies fit, London? My cock was made for you." I'm so turned on and listening to his words is bringing me closer to climax. "This pussy is mine. No one else will ever have it again. Only me. Say it, London. Say it belongs to me."

"My pussy belongs to you, Ezra." His lips crash on mine and we kiss untamed as his strokes take us both to our climax.

The night is full of dirty talk, and we have sex on every surface. By the time we make it to bed to sleep, we can barely move. I am completely exhausted in the best way, feeling totally claimed and realizing that I'm giving my heart to this man. No matter how scary it feels or how fast it seems, I can't think of a better feeling I have ever had. With my head on his chest and him running his fingers through my hair, we both drift into completely satisfied sleep.

Chapter Seven

I know that saying 'see you later' at the airport will be hard. I don't want him to go, but I know after last night that our relationship has turned a corner. We are on our way to something deep and real. I can tell by the way he holds my hand the entire way to the airport, the way he kisses me at every stoplight, and the way we can share a comfortable silence and still be connected. I know after this visit and last night that I am losing myself to this relationship in the best way.

Ezra's leaving from the private airstrip again at RDU, but we say our farewells in the car.

"This is hard. I'll miss waking up next to you," he admits. I put the car in park and turn to him.

"I know, right? But we video chat, text, and talk daily. That's what's on repeat in my head. It's not the same, but we can do this."

"Yes," he says with a kiss, leaning across the center console. Wrapping my arms around his neck, I deepen the kiss, putting all my emotions into my lips.

Breaking the kiss and connecting our foreheads, I remind him, "It's only three weeks of me being here and then I will come to you for a few weeks before heading to Nebraska. LA will be fun; it's my favorite place to visit and be a tourist. You can show me the city through your eyes."

"I can't wait. I will dazzle you."

"Not too much. I mostly just want you. And food." He devours my mouth after that comment. When we come up for air, I am smiling when I say, "And wine."

"You are," he starts before we lose ourselves in another make-out session, "everything I want, London." That sentence will be seared into my soul for all of time.

"You are," I kiss him again deeply and passionately, "everything I need, Ezra." With those last words, he exits the car, and we start the next chapter of this relationship.

* * * *

Week one is hard but manageable. We text a lot and talk multiple times a day. At night, his face on video call is the last thing I see before falling asleep. He sends the most stunning flower arrangement with calla lilies, poppies, celosias, and fire lilies. Attached is a card that says one word:

"Everything."

As he gets busier the calls get shorter, the text responses take longer to come, and our video calls become less frequent. With the time difference, it's tricky, but we manage to work in some creative sexy time. Week two is difficult, but he still sends beautiful flowers. He's making some florist very happy because I get gladioluses, orchids, amaryllises, lotuses, and tulips. My office and home are filled with these beautiful arrangements, and I keep all the sweet notes that come with each delivery. But we both keep missing calls from each other. When we do talk on the phone, it's rushed; I have meetings to go to and he's often distracted by crowds of fans. I can't get his full attention.

By week three, we're both missing each other and being short in our conversations. I'm trying to stay out of my head about him not having time for me or me not wanting the stress that comes with a long-distance relationship. By mid-week of week three, I'm annoyed. I'm trying to get everything scheduled for the months I'm going to be spending in Nebraska and trying to get ready for the trip to LA. The day before I fly out to LA, every possible issue seems to pop up. I'm driving Ami insane, and our new project manager in South Carolina, Elle, is probably having second thoughts about the crazy boss lady.

As I am angrily typing emails in my office, Ami comes in with Elle on the phone about another issue in South Carolina. Ami looks completely done and puts Elle, who is cussing at someone in the background, on speaker, and I only got the end of it. Ami puts the phone on mute and says, "I am so happy we hired Elle; she fits perfectly with us."

I smirk and say, "You're just saying that because she cusses like us."

After a distant "Fuck you, and do your job," Elle comes back to the line.

"Amelia, I wanted you to know that I can handle these stupid fucks in South Carolina, no need for you to come back," Elle assures her. "I will get all the additional permits handled and get these assholes back on schedule."

Ami is smiling when she says, "I have London here with me."

"Oh shit, and I was just cussing like that. Warn a girl."

I decided that I really like Elle too. "No need to censor yourself for me," I tell her. "I like it when my employee has initiative. I'm sending a nice/nasty email to these companies now about all the hold-ups we're getting, and I'm telling them that if they don't get their shit together, I will enforce the fines clauses in our contracts. I have never done it before, but these fuckers are testing my patience."

Elle adds, "I agree. I have been threatening that clause too. I apologize if I jumped the gun, but nothing lights a fire like a 50k fine."

"Agreed."

Ami chimes in. "Are you sure you don't need one of us in South Carolina? The city office can be a political landmine to deal with."

"Don't you worry, I know how to pour on the sugar too," Elle assures us both. After we add a few more fires to Elle's list to put out, she accepts them all and says she can handle it. "I will see you both next month in Nebraska, so we can meet with contractors and city officials."

I know Elle is a single mom and I am doing all I can to make sure travel for work is manageable for her. I ask before we end the call, "Will the travel be manageable with Duke? I know two weeks is a long time to be gone from him."

"He's excited for me to go. I don't know if I like that or not." We all laugh at that statement. "It will work out. I'll book him a flight to come see me on the weekend. He is excited to fly on a plane for the first time."

"That's great news. Hopefully, we can find something fun that he would like to do before he arrives."

Ami finishes the call and then sits across from me as I continue my nice/nasty emails. I glance up from my computer at her and ask, "What? We have lots to do before tomorrow. Is there something else?"

After a beat, she comes out with, "You are so uptight right now. Have you not heard from him?"

"I have heard from him. I'm just busy trying to handle and arrange my schedule for two weeks in LA and then heading straight to Nebraska."

"That sounds like an excuse. Don't pull away from him, London. I know you. You find the smallest issue and then make it bigger in your head. Both of you are busy people, but busy people have time for relationships too."

I stop typing to give her my attention and then place my hands on my head because she is right.

"Ugh. I know. I know. It's just been annoying being away from him and he is always surrounded by so many freaking people. It's like, y'all go do something else, jeez, he's on the phone."

"He won't always be able to empty the room to talk to you. You need to learn to compromise. If you know he is surrounded by people, then have a text convo, not a phone convo."

"So much is lost through text tone."

"Stop fucking overthinking everything. Just have a conversation with the man, whether it's by text or phone."

I'm screaming in my head because I am doing exactly what Ami says I am: dwelling on small things and making them big things. "I hear you," is all I manage to say with a heavy sigh.

"London, do not sabotage this. If there are going to be issues, let them be actual issues, not the number of times you spoke in one week."

"I am so in my head, and I there's been so much time without him that I feel like this will be the normal flow of our relationship. Can I handle this lifestyle? Am I always going to be this needy? Am I too attached already? I don't want to feel this clingy, but I really like him, and I don't want my brain to screw my chances."

"So, don't let it. You control your emotions and your thoughts. Control the things you can and let go of the things you can't. I am sure he wants this to work just as much as you do. Let it work. As the kids say, 'take a chill pill.'"

"No one says that anymore, Ami."

She laughs. "Well, they used to say it."

"I'll work on accepting the things I can control and letting go of the things I can't. That includes with this job. You need to be ready for more responsibility. I'm going to need to lean on you more to travel and manage business relationships. Are you ready for this?"

"I've been ready. I can handle so much more and help with all the ideas we work on together. I can handle bringing them to reality. I am ready, London."

"Okay. This business can't suffer in order for me to have a relationship. If there is an issue that can't be solved without me, that's okay. I'll help solve it. This is my career, my dream job, and I want to keep doing it. I do it well and my team are rockstars."

Amelia agrees with me. "We've got this. We can run this business and have love lives."

"Agreed. You need to start looking for someone to hire as an assistant. Someone who can mostly work in this office but also travel when we need him or her. Wait, you said we can have love lives. Amelia, did you meet someone and not tell me?"

"I would never keep that kind of secret from you. But now that I see how happy you are with Ezra, it's making me want to date again. I think I'll start trying to be more open and remove the big 'fuck off' sign I have on my forehead when men hit on me."

"That makes me happy. Let's start finding you a man while we're in LA."

"LA, really, is that where you go to meet a man?"

"Never know."

"I guess. I'll post a job listing for a new administrative position. It will take some scheduling magic to do interviews, but I will get it done."

"I know you will, Ami. I don't tell you enough, but I value you. You are my best friend and the best employee I could have prayed for. The success of this business is just as much yours as mine. So, thank you. I love you, girl."

"Ew. Control your emotions," Amelia says with a smile on her face. I know she hates it when I thank her for her hard work. As she is leaving my office, she looks back over her shoulder to say, "I love you too," and then she is gone when I look up to smile at her.

We work late, but we get everything set up for the video meetings next week and I manage to put a dent in my email inbox. Amelia will meet me in LA in a few days after she finishes what she needs to do here. Then we will go together to Nebraska. Riding to the airport with Ami gives me more time to go through emails and help Elle with things in South Carolina before I get on the plane.

After the heart-to-heart with Ami, I have been able to get my thoughts under control. I'm working through my own insecurities with communication. Even though Ezra hasn't responded to my texts this morning, I know he received them because he turned on his read receipt in our message thread. I haven't decided if I like that yet, but again, that is my insecurity, not his.

I am flying commercial because I don't have star status, but I did treat myself to a non-stop flight and a first-class ticket. Right when I am boarding the flight, I get a text from Ezra.

"Hurry up and get here already."

That cools my nerves and brings my excitement out. I'm going to see Ezra and that thought brings joy to my heart. I work and sleep on the flight and when I land, the time change is welcome because it feels like I get more time with Ezra. I brought way too much luggage, but I rationalized it with the fact that I am going directly to Nebraska from LA, and I will be there for at least the next eight months. Also, I didn't know what to pack for my time in LA with Ezra as my tour guide. I don't want to be underdressed; a girl needs options.

Once I have retrieved all my luggage and made it to the exit, I find a well-dressed man standing next to the sexiest Lamborghini Urus-S and holding a sign with my name. We see each other at the same time because he walks over to me and says, "Ms. Isle, I am Dein. I will be your driver."

All I can think is that I wonder how he knew me, but then I am reminded of Ezra's star status and that Dein likely had a photo of me. I let Dein take over pushing my luggage and add, "Nice to meet you, Dein. Please call me London."

Dein smiles as he opens the passenger door for me and takes my bookbag, shoulder bag, and carry-on to put in the trunk with all my other luggage. When I get in the backseat, I turn around and say to Dein as he is loading the bags, "I overpacked. Will it all fit?"

He just laughs like this isn't his first time loading this much luggage and says, "Of course, this is no problem, Ms. London." I don't correct him about the "Ms." because at least he used my first name this time.

As I settle into my seat, I notice a gorgeous bouquet of flowers on the backseat beside me with my name on the card. The hand-tied bouquet is a masterpiece and the flowers in it are just as masterful. There are daisies, peonies, roses, hydrangeas, sunflowers, hibiscuses, and heliconia with beautiful greenery to finish. The card is handwritten, and it looks like Ezra's writing. He personalized the note and that makes me happier than getting the flowers does. I open the card and laugh out loud, getting a 'don't be a crazy lady,' look from Dein, but I can't remove the smile from my face. I read the note again,

"Look at the thought put into these flower choices.
I would say all your efforts are required on my cock."

I slide the card into my wallet. I will add it to the collection when I get back to North Carolina. Holding my bouquet and watching LA go past as we head towards the hills, I know two things for a fact: I am falling in love and the 'I missed you sex' is going to be crazy tonight. Fuck me, I better stretch first.

Chapter Eight

The drive to his Malibu mansion is breathtaking. The beautiful lawns, fountains, and sculptures inside the gated community are astonishing. Once inside the circle driveway of the enormous modern ranch mansion, all I can do is stare; seeing how the 1% lives is shocking. I'm just glad Ezra isn't with me to see my jaw-dropping reaction to his home. I've never been in such an extravagant house before and I don't want to look thirsty, as the young people say. When Dein opens my door, I'm able to pick my chin up off the ground and maintain what I hope is only a slightly impressed expression on my face.

"We're here, Ms. London," Dein says as I continue to survey the home where I will be spending the next few weeks. "Mr. Everest is not home yet, but his staff are aware of your arrival, and you are most welcome."

"Thank you, Dein." I manage to stumble out as he is getting my luggage and rolling it up the walkway. Dein and I are greeted at the door by a gentleman, who introduces himself as Larry and says he will be able to help with any household needs I require. He begins to assist Dein with my luggage. Once inside, I realize the front of the house does nothing to prepare you for the views both inside and out of it. The back of the house faces hills with all the natural beauty of God's earthly creations.

As my luggage is being wheeled away, I am pulled to the glass walls where I continue to admire the beauty outside of this house. While I am lost in the view, a throat clears to let me know I am no longer alone. I look to see an older woman with a huge welcoming smile on her face. She extends her hand in greeting. "London, it is so very lovely to meet you. I'm Olga, the house manager."

Her smile is contagious and I can't help but greet her the same way. "It's nice to meet you too, Olga," I return with a huge grin. "This view and house are stunning. I knew Ezra lived well but this is beyond what I imagined, and it is still so welcoming. I can tell this is truly his home."

"One of the best parts of working for Ezra is that he makes this a home and a wonderful place to work," Olga says as she looks past me to the view I have been admiring. "I will take those flowers for you, London, and put them in a vase."

"That would be great, thank you. Would you place it on that beautiful island there?" I point to the island in the open-floor-plan kitchen. I have plans for that bouquet that include standing at the door in nothing but panties and those flowers next to me when Ezra arrives. I leave that last part out since I want to make a great impression on Olga.

"Absolutely. Can I give you a tour? Ezra won't be home for several hours. I can show you where you will be sleeping in case you want to freshen up before he arrives, and I can show you a space to work if you need privacy. I also prepared light snacks for you in case you're hungry."

"Olga, I think we are going to be best friends."

She laughs at me before accepting the flowers and moving toward the kitchen to arrange them in a vase. Olga then guides me through the most beautiful home I have ever seen. She shows me light fixtures, décor, open spaces, huge windows with sweeping views, the pool, gym, and guest suites. She even shows me the back entrance that leads down to the staff quarters when they stay on the property. Olga tells me she doesn't normally live here but when Ezra is in residence, she likes to be available for emergencies. The home is beyond my description of beauty, and I can picture the life that he is building here. I hope that I get to be a part of that life for a long time.

Olga leads me back to the master suite where Ezra and I will sleep and leaves me there. The suite is very soft and masculine with deep blues, greys, and cream colors to decorate the room. Ezra has a huge custom king bed that sits in the far corner of the room facing the floor-to-ceiling windows that take up the entire back wall. I cannot wait to see the sunset from this room. There is an alcove that can be used as a reading nook or a workspace. I knew immediately that this is the area where I will take my business video calls this week. This room is so inviting and comfortable. The ensuite bathroom is the stuff of wet dreams with his and her vanities, a huge tub, and a shower that could fit seven people. I wander to the closet and find the most immaculate layout. It is highly organized with tables, drawers, and a whole section for just jewelry and shoes. I only see a few of his watches in the jewelry section; it's mostly empty and ready for the woman of the house to add her items one day. I want to be that woman, is all I'm thinking as I imagine filling this closet with my stuff too.

My suitcase is already inside the closet. I make my way over to open it to get my things out to shower and to prepare for Ezra's arrival home. After I've finished freshening up, checked emails, and returned calls, I make my way back to the kitchen and have a few of the snacks that Olga left for me. I know I still have some time before he comes home but I can't wait to hear his voice anymore, so I go sit on the back patio and call Ezra. He answers on the first ring.

"Hey, honey."

"Babe. Your house is beyond amazing and Olga, Larry, and Dein have been so great."

"I'm glad you like it and them. They have been a godsend for me."

"I really do. Everything about it is beautiful and the views…Ezra, seriously. I love it."

I can hear the smile in his voice when he says, "I can't wait to see you. I probably have another hour on this set before I can leave. Traffic to get home will be horrible because it's LA."

"That's okay, good-looking. I'm just going through all your stuff and leaving little pieces of me everywhere so anyone who comes in will know a woman has been here."

"Only you have been there. I don't normally have guests at that house. I use another place for that."

"Good answer, Ezra."

"True answer, London."

"Thank you for my flowers. I love them too."

"Good."

I take a deep breath, just holding the phone to my ear and listening to him breathe. He says something to someone in the background about hurrying up because he wants to go home. I can't help the smile on my face knowing that this man is eager to get to me.

"Baby, I am going to finish this as quickly as possible," he says. "I'll see you soon, London."

"I can't wait, honey," I say before we end our phone call and I head back into the house. Olga is preparing dinner and it looks amazing.

"Olga, do you need my help with dinner?" I ask.

She looks at me with surprise in her eyes and smiles before saying, "No, London, but thank you for offering."

"No problem. I'll just be in the living room if you need me."

"Okay. I'm going to put this meal in the crockpot and then get out of here so you can have the house to yourselves."

"Thank you," is all I say as I make my way into the other room.

A while later, Olga comes into the living room to say her goodbyes and let me know all the staff have left the house. After she shows me what door Ezra will enter through, she exits for the evening. I head back to the bedroom to put on my 'welcome home and I have missed you' outfit for Ezra. I put on a sexy maroon matching bra and panties that are going to end up on the floor in the kitchen, but I bought them to wear for Ezra and I can't wait to see his face when he sees them. The sexy thong barely covers my honey pot, and the bra has the sexiest cutouts. After making sure I am smooth and shiny, I put on my fuck-me black Manolos to set off the sexy lingerie and sit at the kitchen island waiting for Ezra. I am scrolling through more of my never-ending emails when I hear the garage open and his car rolling in. I put my phone on silent and put it away. I move to stand directly in his line of sight when he opens the door and adjust the beautiful flower arrangement beside me so he can see both of us when he enters. I am already so wet just thinking of him touching me when he sees these heels and this lingerie.

I heard the car turn off, the garage shut, and the car door closing. He is talking on the phone, but I hear him say, "I'm hanging up now because I'm home," before he reaches the door.

The entry door opens, and our eyes meet. He glances at the flowers beside me but then slowly takes in what I am wearing as he comes inside and closes the door. He is taking in every inch of fabric, skin, and heels.

"Hey, London," he says in a low, sexy voice as he drops his items on the counter and moves closer to me with dirty thoughts behind his eyes.

"Welcome home, Ezra. I'm so happy to see you." He moves completely into my space, only inches from me as I greet him.

He licks his lips before saying, "What a welcome, you in my kitchen in this and those heels, next to the flowers I got you. My home has never looked so good." He is running his fingers along my skin and is so close to my lips without kissing me. He keeps going with his sexy talking, asking, "Are you already wet for me?" He licks my lips before I can answer him and leans down to run his lips up my neck while running his fingers around the front of my stomach, right at the top of my panties.

"Yes, I can't wait to have your cock."

"Oh, honey." He slips his fingers inside the top of my panties and moved down to my folds before saying, "I can't wait to give you my cock." He uses his other hand to tease my nipples through the fabric of the bra. "You are so fucking sexy and wet, London."

I moan as he slips his fingers inside me and kisses me breathless. We come up for air and he has my bra undone and off me, his mouth closing over my nipple. I move my hands to his shirt, ready to undress him. "Babe, you are wearing too many clothes."

He must agree because he lifts his mouth from my nipple long enough to remove his shirt. I immediately touch his body and make my way to his belt to get his pants off next. As he toes off his shoes and we work to get him naked, his mouth never leaves my skin. He is pushing his dick against me as he rips the thong to get it off. We are all kisses, hands, and moans when he breaks away and turns me around, rubbing his dick against my ass. "This is going to be hard and fast, London. I have been hard the whole drive home thinking of your tight pussy on my dick and then I open the door and find you in this in my kitchen."

He pushes me down on the counter, spreads my legs, and enters me at the same time. We both curse in sync, "Fuck." He keeps slamming into me, pumping faster.

"Come on, Ezra, give it to me," I moan. "Harder, I won't break."

He slaps my ass and pulls my hair as he pounds into me harder while I grip the counter to hold on for the ride. He was right, it is fast because it's only a few more strokes before he is cursing, "London, fuck, I'm coming." He is still deep inside of me as he kisses my spine and shoulders, whispering how much he missed me and how happy he is that I'm here. I stand up and turn around to wrap my arms around him and we stand in the kitchen naked and kissing as his cum runs down my thighs.

We are still touching and rubbing each other as I tell him about my arrival, house tour, and how much I missed him. I reach down to wrap my hands around his cock, which is still wet with my juices, squeezing and pumping him until he is ready to go again. I take his hand, lean him against the floor-to-ceiling window, and drop to my knees.

I look up at him. "The moment I saw this view, the only thing I could think was that I was going to suck your dick with this view in the background."

I do just that; I take him deep in my throat, licking and sucking him. I relax my jaw and open my throat when he takes control and fucks my mouth. I feel so powerful watching this influential man come apart in my mouth. I take all of him and when he comes, I swallow all of it.

We spend hours having sex and talking in the living room before having the dinner that Olga left for us. After multiple orgasms, pure exhaustion takes hold, and we fall asleep with his cock still inside of me in his king bed as dawn lightens the sky.

Chapter Nine

Over the next several days, Ezra and I spent lots of time together. He works from home when he can, and I find a nice spot to hold a video meeting with my team about our updates in South Carolina and starting the project in Nebraska. I love my team. I can't say it enough. Even when I'm on the other side of the country, they still operate like a well-oiled machine.

Ezra treats me to the real LA/Hollywood experience when we're not having sex, taking meetings, or having deep conversations that really show how much I'm losing my heart to this man. We do helicopter tours, private meals with Michelin star chefs, private beach dinners, shopping on Rodeo Drive, a private movie screening, private tours of the Getty and Griffith Observatory, and meals at so many good restaurants. We take his Ferrari for a ride down the 101 up the coastline; the view is spectacular. Watching the sunset in a private cove makes it the perfect movie setting and we make out like a pair of teenagers. I am truly having the best time with him; we have so much in common and I am very surprised. I realize that I really like who he is, so genuine, caring, funny, and sexy as fuck, and our morals and life values align. We are both spiritual, and he is truly the best sexual partner I have ever had. It isn't just about the sex, either; I am quickly realizing it's the intimacy that matters the most, something I have never felt before, but the experience makes the orgasms stronger and last longer. I don't know how any man could follow him because, for me, I know I am looking at my forever.

* * * *

My visit with him is coming to an end and he decides he wants me to attend a friend's dinner with him. He explains that it's Adam and Pam and they have been great friends for more than fifteen years. He talks about how he and Adam were inseparable when he arrived in LA. After meeting at a commercial audition, they quickly became real friends. Ezra says Adam never got his big break in Hollywood and moved on from trying to be an actor, instead becoming a very successful engineer. When I tell him I would love to meet his family, because it sounds like Adam and Pam are family, he tells me that they live an hour and a half north of LA.

He wants to show me the condo downtown that he uses most of the time because it's closer to set. He admits to me that no woman he ever dated has been to the house in Malibu except me and that makes me feel very special.

After spending the morning getting couples massages and then shopping in tacky tourist stores for me to get gifts for my team, we finish the day with more shopping. All day, we have been flirting, sneaking kisses, and slight touches; it's basically hours of foreplay, and by the time we get to his condo, I'm ready to strip naked and let him take me on every surface. I think he will, but he keeps up the slow burn, showing me the kitchen and living area. When he goes to open the patio door, I stop him by grabbing his belt, pulling him to me, and connecting our lips. I open my mouth to let him deepen the kiss.

When it slows, I say, without disconnecting my lips from his, "Enough. I want you now." I need him before I have to get ready to meet his best friends. It will help release some of the pent-up nerves I'm secretly harboring.

As his smile grows against my lips, he says, "You only have to ask, baby."

I want him in this living room, but he starts leading me backward down a hallway, telling me he wants us in a bed. We're all hands and lips as we back down the hall. I run my hands up his shirt to remove it and he removes mine too. He kicks a door open with his foot as we throw our shirts on the floor and kiss each other with every emotion we share. My hands are working their way into his pants when I hit the edge of the bed, and he pushes me onto it. I sit down using my hands to keep me from lying back. Then I reached back up to put my palm on his abs and unbuckle his belt.

But Ezra is no longer responding to my touch and when I look up to meet his eyes, they're not looking at me but at whatever is over our shoulders. His gaze is full of shock, fear, and terror. I follow his gaze to look over my shoulder and that's when I realize what's causing the pure panic radiating from him. I realize my backside is wet and when I look at the palm touching Ezra, I see it's covered in red. That red has left my handprint directly on his abs where I was touching him. Behind me is a beautiful but very dead woman.

Ezra backs away immediately, still with shock on his face and panic about to rip through him.

"Oh my god," is all I get out before I jump from the bed, which is soaked in her blood. I turn to him and ask, "Is this for a scene or props?"

Ezra doesn't answer me.

"Is she someone from set who's trying to get your attention?"

Ezra continues to stare but manages to shake his head no. The beautiful dead woman is a redhead with stunning green eyes that are now lifeless. She's dressed in a beautiful summer dress and lying in the middle of the bed Ezra and I were about to have sex in. The redhead had slit her wrists and used the blood to write on the white headboard, "Why her?" and then collapsed there and died. I check her for a pulse just to be sure she's dead. The one thing about me is that I'm great in a crisis, and right now Ezra needs me to be the problem solver because he can't get the pain and panic off his face.

My backside and hands are covered in the blood I sat in, but I wipe my palms on my jeans as I quickly make my way to the front room, dragging Ezra along with me. He doesn't need to keep staring at the dead body. I'm peppering him with questions.

"Do you know her?"

"How did she get in?"

"Is she an ex?"

"Do you think she's a stalker of yours?"

"Are you sure you have never seen her?"

"Could she be working on the set of your current movie?"

All he says is, "There is a dead woman in my bed. Her wrists were slit."

I am sure he's going into shock, so I get him a bottle of water and grab my phone off the counter to start getting help. I lead Ezra to the kitchen table and direct him to drink water while I start making calls. I have his phone as well and use his face to open it up because he's still not speaking, but he is drinking the water. I hover close by him because my clothes have blood all over them and I don't want it to be all over the apartment. Ezra and I have already been in the room and tainted any evidence, so I think it would be best if I didn't put the blood anywhere else.

Using Ezra's phone, I use the map app to pull up the address of our current location. I call the non-emergency police dispatcher first because the woman is already dead. She wasn't that cold, though, and there was no dead person smell in the condo because we would have noticed that immediately when we entered. When the dispatcher comes to the phone I state, "Hello, this is London Isle, I am at 78900 Boulevard of Stars, in the penthouse apartment. I would like to report a dead body inside my boyfriend's house. I checked her pulse but there wasn't one. There is a lot of blood all over the bed and a message on the headboard. There are also deep cuts to both her wrists all the way to her elbows."

I am surprised at how calm I am, but I get out all the details and answer the dispatcher's questions. Lastly, I request, "Please send the most discreet detectives. I don't know your protocol, but my boyfriend is a very big A-list movie star, whose name I won't say on a recorded line. I don't want fan cops showing up at this scene."

The dispatcher advises that they have a protocol, and she will enact it right now. She wants me to stay on the phone with her, so I put her on speaker and then use Ezra's phone to call his business manager, who will know what attorney to call. I don't know much about Ezra's manager, only that his name is William. When I dial him, he answers with, "What can I do for my favorite client?"

I answered by introducing myself. "Hey William, my name is London. I'm the girlfriend. We have a major issue at the

Boulevard of Stars condo. This issue is going to require the LAPD. He's in shock right now and not saying much, but I'm pretty sure that because of who he is you have a plan for an event like this. If so, now is a great time to execute said plan." I didn't use Ezra's name because the other phone line was still open and the police are listening.

William is quiet for a moment, probably trying to get his thoughts together, before he responds, "Did you already call the police?"

"The police were my first call from my personal cell and the dispatcher is still on the line with me on my phone. I'm calling you not on speaker."

He sighs heavily like he wished I had not called the police first, but that is tough luck because not calling the cops first is not the way this girl handles a crisis. That is the shit that gets people arrested.

William begins speaking. "Okay, don't let Ezra make a statement."

"Well, that's obvious," I say a little snippily, but then I take a breath and apologize. "Sorry, yes, no statement. What else?"

He continues, "I will call his attorney and if he doesn't make it to the condo in time, he will meet you at the station. They take movie stars to certain stations to complete questioning and his attorney, Devin, will meet you there."

"Okay. Sounds good."

"Stay with them the whole time. Do not let them take photos of Ezra."

"Okay."

"Don't give them too much information. Make sure they know his attorney is on the way. You should probably call your attorney too. If you can afford one."

Clearly, Ezra is not close with his business manager because this man doesn't know I'm not some poor out-of-work loser trying to take Ezra's fame and money. So, I give him an attitude that I do not apologize for. "Well, since I have a net worth of more than eight million dollars, yes, I can afford my own fucking attorney, you asshole." I hung up the phone on William, hoping to never meet him.

Once the police arrive, everything moves in a blur. I'm holding both my phone and Ezra's because I don't want anyone to swipe it by 'accident.' I am photographed by the techs because I have the redhead's blood all over me. They take a shot of my handprint on Ezra's stomach, which I supervise and ensure there are no shots with his face or any distinguishing marks. When the police try to talk with Ezra, I hold his hand as I repeat to them that he will make a statement once his attorney arrives, but let them know I would be happy to speak with them. I tell them the events that unfolded and don't leave out a single detail. When they ask me to step away so they can talk to Ezra in private, I decline and advise them he won't have any conversations without his attorney present.

As if I summoned him, I heard a loud voice come from the hallway advising the LAPD they will be facing a very large fine if they don't let him in with his client. I tell the police officer speaking with me that his attorney is Devin and that I believe that's him in the hallway. Devin is insistent that he get in and finally, while I continue to stop the cops from probing into unrelated areas of his home, they let the attorney onto the scene.

Devin takes one look at me and the blood before pulling out files for the detective. He introduces himself and then provides the police with six files on stalkers that Ezra currently has. Devin advises that these six are the most likely to have done something like break into his home. Devin also tells the police that the LAPD has been made aware of these stalkers but, according to their criteria, it doesn't meet the level of action required to monitor them. The detective accepts the file and then asks me to give my statement again.

I take a deep breath and repeat for the fifth time, "We spent the day doing regular stuff together. He was showing me his city, and then we came here to freshen up before our dinner plans with his friends, Adam and Pam. Ezra was giving me a tour of the apartment. We stopped touring before we got out of the living room and headed to the bedroom to have sex.

While in the midst of removing our clothing, we managed to make it to the bed, where Ezra, in a sexy gesture, pushed me onto the bed. Completely non-violent push." I add that last part to make sure they don't try to make the push into something it was not. "I used my hand to break my fall." I show the blood on my palm. "I reached up to touch Ezra, placing my hand on his stomach." I point to the handprint on his stomach. "I realized he was stiff and no longer focused on me. He was staring over my shoulder at something that was shocking and terrifying. I looked over my shoulder and that is when I saw the redhead, lying there dead. I looked at the headboard and saw the message. Ezra backed away from the bed, still in shock. I got up, walked around the bed, and placed two fingers on the redhead's neck to feel for a pulse. No pulse was found. I wiped my bloodied hand on my jeans, grabbed Ezra, and then we came into the kitchen where I called the police first. Then I contacted Ezra's business manager. As you can see, detectives, my story has not changed and will not change."

The older detective asks me, "Why are you so calm? You don't look to be in shock at all. You have clear recall of your day and, as you pointed out, your story has not changed even the slightest."

I look him dead in the eye and say, "Not sure why it matters, but I happen to be great in a crisis. I can freak out later when I don't have an audience. Also, this is not my first time finding a suicide victim."

At that comment, Ezra turns his head to me, and I can see the questions in his eyes. We've talked about so much, but that story is one I have not told anyone but Amelia, and it took eight years of friendship before I told her. That story is not one I like or want to share, but from the look in his eyes, it seems that Ezra wants to understand why I would keep something like that from him. It isn't anger in his eyes, more like confusion about why he didn't know that fact about me. I hate telling the sad story, but I will; I will tell him when the moment is right. But not in a room full of strangers.

At that moment, the detective asks, "Do you want to elaborate?"

I simply state, "No."

Devin jumps in, saying, "I think all the stories for today have been told, gentlemen. If you folks can finish up, I know Ezra and London want to get out of this condo."

Truer words have never been spoken. I squeeze Ezra's hand, lending him more support because he's still very confused about why this has happened. But I can see him coming back and he's getting pissed. I bet he did not know about these stalkers. I would also bet he didn't know about the reports of the stalkers being sent to the police. And I would bet my last dime that he was wondering exactly how his condo address was leaked, and how this redhead got into his apartment. I think his team has a mole, but would someone really give out his home address, especially to someone with mental health issues? Someone that could have potentially been very dangerous to Ezra?

The crime scene techs wrap up, taking all the evidence they need, including the clothes I was wearing, and then the medical examiner arrives and removes the redhead from the bedroom. In all, it's after 2 a.m. when we make it back to the Malibu house. Ezra is able to regain his focus without having to go to the hospital. He backs my story with the police multiple times. Then he gets us to his home safely and I get ready for bed on autopilot.

When I get in the bed next to him, he puts his arm around me, and I finally feel it all. With Ezra standing strong again, I'm able to fall apart, which is exactly what I do, crying and sobbing into his chest, asking why someone would take their own life when there is so much to live for. Through all the tears, shaking, anger, disbelief, and more tears, Ezra just holds me and speaks soft, kind words. He tells me how he couldn't have made it through this without me, how he is so blessed to have me, how he never wants me to leave, and repeatedly how strong I am. He reminds me that we will get through this together. That we can get through anything together.

Chapter Ten

I wake with a headache after crying myself to sleep. I find Ezra wrapped around me and still fast asleep when I look over at him. After untwining myself from him, I make my way to the bathroom. I can see the puffy eyes and dark circles beneath them, the results of an emotional night. I wash my face and brush my teeth before leaving the bathroom. Then I crawl back into bed with Ezra. He reaches for me as soon as I am back in bed and kisses my shoulder once he has me close enough. My mind is already running through yesterday's events, and I know that I will not be able to go back to sleep, so I lie in thought while Ezra holds me.

It seems like a while passes before he fully wakes and heads to the bathroom only to come back and cuddle with me again in bed. These cuddles are one of my favorite things about waking up with him. Also, I appreciate the fact that he is already sporting morning wood and I can't wait to satisfy him. When I roll over to kiss him good morning, however, I can see that he is deep in thought.

"Good morning, baby," I say.

"Good morning," he says, but before I can kiss him, he continues. "London, you said yesterday that it wasn't your first time discovering a victim of suicide?" He has a look of tenderness in his eyes. He wants to know my secrets, the good and the bad, and I find myself wanting to tell him.

"Yes." I exhale quietly. "I found my roommate years ago. She had slit her wrists. I found her in her bed," I tell him with a shaky, quiet voice.

He inhales sharply, "Baby, that is horrible. What happened?"

I hate telling this story and I haven't spoken of it in many years because of the trauma it caused me. I can feel myself trying to pull away from him because of the sting. I don't want to relive that horrible day and I don't want him to look at me differently.

Before I can turn away, he pulls me closer to him and kisses me softly, saying in a low voice, "I want to know. I want to know all of you. Even the things that scare you. Don't pull away now. Tell me anyway."

I roll on my back and look at the ceiling as the tears slip uncontrollably from my eyes. I want him to know this, not only because I am falling for him, but because he will need to know, especially if the police ask more questions. With a steady breath, I tell Ezra about the worst day of my life. It feels like I am removed from the beautiful bedroom, and I am right back in the apartment I shared with Piper.

"My roommate, Piper, struggled with depression for a long time," I tell him. "She was getting treatment and taking her medication. She was always transparent with me about her struggles. We discussed her therapy, how she was doing, life, boys, sex, everything and anything; we were very close friends. It's crazy because we went to the same college but had never met until we moved in with each other. She posted a flyer at the school, and I called. We laughed about all the crazy people who had applied. We clicked instantly and I knew it would be a perfect rooming situation.

"One night, after living together for about three months, Piper told me about her struggles with depression, and I told her about the emotional abuse I'd endured from my parents. The fact that we both had problems connected us on a deeper friendship level. After that conversation, we were inseparable. I was just starting my company and she was working as a manager for a high-end restaurant, so we got busy, and our talks fell off and became phone and text chats instead of face-to-face ones for an extended period. But we tried to do dinner a few times a month.

"I don't know when things got so bad for Piper. I only remember that at one point I was constantly absent because of all the things I was trying to get going. I was leaving home by 5:30 a.m. and getting home after midnight. I was listening to all these business growth podcasts and audiobooks, and reading personal growth books. I was being selfish because I knew Piper needed me to decompress, but I didn't want her energy, which was often more negative than positive, to bring down my vibes. It was so stupid, self-centered, and mean. My best friend in the whole world suffered from depression and here I was worried about how to find more seed money for my startup and which property I should buy and whether my business plan was detailed enough. I should have been more present for her."

I take a deep breath before I continue. "We had a big fight a week before she did it. We yelled at each other and said hurtful things. The worst part is now I don't even remember what we argued about. The night before she died, I had to take a slow day because I was so exhausted and running myself down. I came home early, and she was home because she took the day off work. We talked and apologized to each other. Piper seemed so happy and talked about the good stuff going on at work. She told me about the progress she was making at therapy. She talked about how happy she was that we found each other and how our living situation was the best she could have wished for. How proud she was of me for starting my business and how successful she knew I would be. How she couldn't believe the amount of work I was doing to get my business going and she encouraged me to keep grinding and that it was all going to pay off.

"We talked about everything and nothing at the same time. It was just like old times, because no matter what we were still bonded and best friends. We watched a movie and I fell asleep. She ordered us the biggest steaks for dinner, and we had this really great wine. I don't remember what it was now; I just know it was the best dinner I had in a long time. It was the best evening. Just me and Piper."

I don't want to continue, but I force myself to go on. "I made sure to sleep in the next morning because I was trying to take a small break, but I got up to make us coffee. Just like we used to before I went to work because her days would sometimes start late in the restaurant business. I made the coffee exactly the way we liked it. Mine was dark and sweet, Piper's light and bitter. That was our inside joke. I opened her bedroom door, said, 'Good morning, coffee time," and I saw her on the bed in her beautiful night dress with her wrist slit and blood everywhere.

"Everything gets spotty after that. I remember the coffee hitting the floor, but not the feel of the burns that covered my wrist that the EMS providers treated me for. I remember screaming and yelling at the 911 operator to send help. I remember the detectives throwing questions at me, but I don't remember my answers. I remember them taking a letter from my hands, but I don't remember what it said. I remember the emptiness I felt after she was wheeled away in a body bag. I remember waking up in a hospital room and crying for a week straight. I remember the pure heartbreak that her parents experienced and them trying to hold me and themselves together while we buried Piper. I remember shutting out everyone after Piper's funeral. I remember promising myself I would never be that broken again, which is how I am able to stay laser-focused during a crisis now. The thing that makes me the saddest is knowing that she spent the night before saying goodbye to me, but the only vivid detail I have of Piper still in my brain is her in that lavender night dress surrounded by blood.

"The police gave the suicide note to her parents in the end, hoping they would get closure. I thought that was the worst thing they could have done. But, when they read her note, they smiled, handed it to me, and cried even more. I didn't read it until a year later, although I am told that I read it when I found her and read it to the 911 operator."

I close my eyes and recite the letter, every word of which is burned into my memory.

London,

You saved me so many times. This has been the most exciting part of my life. Don't let this destroy you. Mourn me. Miss me every once in a while. Remember me like we were last night. I have never had a friend like you, and I am always with you. Just not in this life anymore. Do better than me. Be happy. Be a Boss Bitch.

Tell my parents it wasn't their fault. I was ready and they were the best parents ever.

I love you, and don't you forget it.

Piper.

"I can still see that letter. No matter how much she didn't want her actions to affect me, they did. I buried myself in work and my business after I read that letter. I made sure the only thing I could think about was my business and how to get to the level of success I wanted. Lots of therapy later and I've learned to accept Piper's choice to end her life. I learned it wasn't my fault. I've learned to find a healthy balance between work and personal life. I learned that it is okay for me to let go of her and move on, that this one event in my life doesn't have to affect my whole life. Piper was a very important chapter in my story, but she isn't my whole book. I learned that saying that out loud doesn't make me a bad person and it doesn't take away from her memory."

I come back from that sad tale with a shake of my head and tears still rolling down my face. When I turn to look into Ezra's eyes, I see they're glassy with my tale.

"Honey, I am so sorry you had to experience that kind of loss," he tells me. "I am proud of you for enduring it and I bet Piper is proud of you too."

Hearing him say that brings a smile to my face. It's good to talk about my dark parts with this man. I am skimming my fingers over his face when I say, "I'm sorry you had to experience that type of trauma too, baby. It isn't something I would wish on my worst enemy. But I will be with you every step of the way. I will help you through this; whatever path it takes, I'll stay with you." Ezra grabs my hand and brings it to his mouth for a kiss. I remind him, "This next part is going to be hard. There'll be so much police questioning. I'm sure your legal team will manage most of it but there will be parts they can't handle. The sadness you may feel or the anger … I'm here for it all."

"We will do this together," he says out loud to reassure himself and me.

"Yes, together." I kiss him softly and he deepens the kiss. It is the most love-filled kiss he has given me. He worships my body with the slow and soft love we make until we both climax while staring deeply into each other's eyes.

* * * *

The morning starts with a sad tale and the day doesn't get any better. We get ready and then leave to go to Ezra's business office to discuss how to proceed with his legal team and business manager. We walk into the office holding hands because it has been one of those mornings where we haven't wanted to let go of each other. Ezra's business suite is so nice and corporate, with all the wood, exposed beams, and tan colors. All the meeting rooms are encased in glass and a few offices line the back walls. I look up to find Ami walking towards me with sheer purpose on her face and she wraps us both in her arms in a hug filled with her love. She kisses us both on the cheek before letting go. Then she puts on her business face. She turns to a beautiful curvy woman, who's wearing a tailored suit that accentuates her figure perfectly. Her hair is styled in the most beautiful dreadlocks, and she looks both friendly and professional.

"London, this is Danielle, your lawyer," Amelia says. "Amira sent her."

"Hello Danielle, I'm London," I say as I shake her hand. "And this is Ezra."

She reaches to shake his hand too. I let go of his other hand to hug Amelia again because she always does everything she can to take care of me. She has this situation all under control and we aren't even at home. Amelia is truly the best person I could have on my team and in my life.

After I release her from the hug, Ezra laces his fingers back through mine as we continue to support each other.

A throat clears and the voice I yelled at on the phone yesterday speaks. "Ezra, if we can go into the conference room, the legal team is ready for you." He begins to lead us to the room and William's eyes widen when he sees me following before saying, "This is best discussed alone."

I fucking hate William and his side-eye looks. With a roll of my eyes, I begin to unlace my hand from Ezra's, but he tightens his hold before saying, "Will, we are doing this together, no need for private meetings. This happened to both of us, and London is my girlfriend."

William is about to argue more, but Ezra gives him a look I have never seen before, and whatever that look is shuts Will up because we breeze right past him into the conference room with Amelia and Danielle following.

The meeting went as expected. We have to tell the same story that we told the cops to Ezra's legal team, William, Amelia, and Danielle. Danielle makes sure to jump in with questions where she sees fit. She challenges Ezra's legal team when she doesn't see their interests working out best for me.

Ezra's legal team informs us that the redhead was identified as one of Ezra's most dedicated stalkers. They'd had a file on her for a long time but didn't realize she would do something as drastic as this. Ezra has been listening quietly, but when his management team begins to explain their prior knowledge of the stalker, he loses his shit.

"Why the fuck was I in the dark about the seriousness of this stalker?" he demands. "Why didn't anyone warn me that I was being followed? How can you be so careless?"

William responds with, "Ez, calm down. You receive lots of stalker-ish letters, emails, and gifts regularly, and we don't like to tell you about everyone. It comes with your profession."

William seems unimpressed by Ezra's reaction and that sets him off. I haven't heard him raise his voice before, but my man stands up for himself; he is not some pretty face who will be taken advantage of. He is not just the 'talent.'

"Calm down? The fuck, Will. Don't tell me to calm down. London was re-traumatized by finding a body in my fucking apartment. I was traumatized. I am angry and fucking pissed that this would happen. It happened in my private home, where I was supposed to be secure and safe. Where the building management assured me of safety and privacy because of who I am. How did she get into the condo? Calm down. What the actual fuck, William? I pay you entirely too much money for me to be worrying about shit like this. I paid entirely too much money for that condo to be experiencing shit like this, too. If the next words out of your mouth are 'calm down,' I will fire everyone in this room."

Well shit, if that wasn't hot.

William thinks before he starts speaking again, but I am ignoring his words because there is a girl in the corner who is either extremely angry or extremely scared. She looks like she wants to say something but has been warned or bullied into not speaking. I only catch the end of William's words, "… these types of things happen to celebrities in your position. It's no one's fault."

I see red and rage is oozing in my words as I snap, "No one's fault? That is absolutely not true, William. Ezra was in serious danger, so much so that his legal team had moved this girl into a folder to submit to law enforcement, and you didn't see fit to warn him? That's completely careless on your part." I jump up out of my chair and everyone stands. "I need five," I say as I storm out of the room before I really lose my shit on good old William.

I walk to the back of the office space, quickly realizing it sucks having glass walls when you are pissed and just want to scream. So, I pace back and forth until Ezra comes to stand in front of me and rubs my arms and back. He tells me, "I have never wanted to fuck you so badly. Your anger has my dick hard."

I laugh out loud, and it releases the tension in my shoulders and brings a smile to my face. "We can role-play the angry boss and employee meeting later tonight," I say.

He kisses me. "Promises, promises. I will expect you to keep that one and wear glasses while we role-play that."

"You got it, love," I say as I observe William's hostile body language while he speaks to the girl I noticed in the meeting. She looks terrified as he whisper-screams at her. Ezra follows my gaze and is visibly pissed at what he sees.

"What the fuck?" is all he says as he moves back in the direction of the meeting room. I see Danielle and Amelia both shooting angry eyes at William and the way he is making this girl cower. We are all back in the conference room when Ezra enters saying, "Why are you talking to her in such a hostile manner?"

William looks up, just noticing that everyone is back in the room and seeing what is happening. "Oh, it's not related, Ez. I'm not speaking to her in any manner other than professionally, right, Rose?"

Everyone turns to Rose, and we can all see the fear in her eyes. I jump in, saying, "Don't do that. Don't use your tone to make her feel threatened."

William turns angry eyes on me. "This is not your concern. You are not a part of this. You're just his flavor of the month. We don't even need to commit your name to memory."

Ami and I both are just about to explode, but Ezra puts his hands on our shoulders to stop us and with the most menacing voice he says, "Get the fuck out, William, now."

He turns to Ezra and says, "You can't be serious, for fuck's sake. She's just a warm pussy."

Ezra says with complete rage, "Now!"

Everyone in the room looks away from William because I imagine they have never seen Ezra this angry before. William turns to his team. "Let's go now," he says, clearly angry with them.

Ezra jumps in. "Not them, just you. Out now."

William storms out of the glass office, to the elevator, and down out of our sight. I mutter, "What a twat," and everyone laughs to lighten the mood.

Ezra turns to Rose to say, "I apologize for never noticing how rude and hostile he was to you." He looks around at William's whole team. "To all of you." They all breathe a collective sigh of relief.

I ask, "What is going on? What was he trying to silence you about, Rose?"

I can tell she is unsure if she should say anything, but she squares her shoulders and decides she is going to speak.

"We all warned William about this woman and how she was sending in photos that were too close and intimate of you, Mr. Everest. As soon as we got letters from her about you dating someone, we told him again to act because it was escalating. William ignored us. We tried to contact you directly but by the time we got the nerve up to go around William, it was too late. We should have acted sooner." She says that last part with defeat and disappointment.

Instead of blaming Rose and the rest of the group, Ezra asks, "Has all the information you collected been provided to Devin and the police?"

Rose says immediately, "Yes, William just didn't want you aware of the amount of evidence we turned over and the fact that we were warning him."

"Okay. So, going forward, when a situation like this happens, do not wait to go around William. I pray this never happens again, but I would rather you be wrong and overreacting than for us to have this type of meeting again. Do you understand?"

They all say in unison, "Yes, sir."

He diffused the situation perfectly, and I shouldn't have expected anything less. This man is humble and understanding in all the right ways. He dismisses the team and assures them that he will deal with William and for them not to worry. I hope he does, but I have a few four-letter words for William if Ezra can't bring himself to tell him on his own.

After such a tense and stressful meeting, Ezra takes Amelia and me to a coffee truck that he swears makes the best coffee and blueberry muffins in the world. The coffee truck is set up at different locations on different days, so you have to follow their app to know where they are. Once we find them near a park, Amelia and I get Ezra's order while he finds a spot for us to sit. Coffee and muffins in hand, we are ready to debrief about the situation at the picnic table Ezra has picked for us. After we all get our first sips of coffee heaven, we all heave a collective sigh, and Amelia pulls out her tablet. She looks at us over her coffee cup and before taking another gulp says, "That was a very fucking negative meeting."

Looking at her, I say, "It really was a sad and negative meeting, but necessary. At least the legal team and Ezra's public relations team know what to do and where to go from here. Thank you for hiring me an attorney, Amelia; you are always so on point. Best assistant/manager/future CEO/friend ever. I don't know if they have mugs that say that, but I'll try to find you one."

Amelia smiles into her cup. Ezra looks between us, watching our work/friendship dynamic. Amelia moves me along with, "So, I have been able to push everything back for one week in Nebraska. All of our items have been sent to the corporate townhouse rental, but I moved all the appointments I could. Some I couldn't move, but I did push them to virtual instead of in person. You can stay here in California with Ezra for another week."

"Okay, that works for me. What about you, babe?" I ask to be sure it works for him.

Ezra pulls up the calendar on his phone and agrees with everything Amelia is saying. He adds, "I want you here as long as possible, and that keeps us from spending a week apart before I can get to Nebraska. But I do have a red-carpet movie premiere event on Saturday. It's for my upcoming romantic comedy. It's the movie adaption of the D. Perry book series."

"Okay, that's fine. I'll find something to do on Saturday while you're at the event. Or I can fly to Nebraska on Saturday, get settled before starting with contractors and meetings on…" I look over at Amelia to tell me the day.

"Tuesday," she provides.

"On Tuesday," I repeat like we are not both sitting at the table with Amelia and can't hear what she says.

"Why would you leave on Saturday?" Ezra asks. "Can't you go with me to the event?"

"Um, I don't know. Are you asking me? Also, you said D. Perry, as in one of the most amazing romance writers ever?"

"What are we, sixteen? I need to ask my girlfriend to attend a party with me? And yes, I believe we are talking about the same person, a very nice lady. I met her a few times."

"When my boyfriend is such a huge movie star whose brand is the fact that he is unattainable and forever sexy and single, I would say yes, I will wait for the invitation. And I am so amazed that you met her, I love all her books. Can you tell us which series or book the movie is based on, or is it a secret?" I love how we are having two conversations at the same time. You know, multi-tasking.

"Well, this boyfriend wants you there and my brand will work around it. Also, are you star-struck by the author? Because I feel like I should be jealous; you didn't make this big of a deal about me and I am a fucking superhero," he says with a smile that reaches his eyes. He has officially seen my 'fan-girl' moment.

As we are discussing this Amelia is typing away, using her skills to make sure I can have what I need to be ready on Saturday. Without looking up from her computer, Amelia says the words on the tip of my tongue, "Obviously you have never read any of her books. That woman is a great storyteller."

"I would love to be your plus one, honey," I say. "You're always my plus one. Also, I am your biggest fan too. I can't believe I get to have sex with the star from her book." I give him a sexy smile with a look that says I can't wait to see him naked again.

"Good comeback, London."

"Amelia, can I have everything I need on such short notice?" I asked her.

Amelia is still typing away when she starts to speak. "Yes, you can. I scheduled a designer to come show you some red-carpet dresses on Thursday. We can do it at my hotel suite; you really went above and beyond with the hotel booking this time, London," Amelia says with a knowing smile on her face since she booked her own room with a company card.

With a smile in my voice, I turned to gaze at her. "Did I? Above and beyond. You know how to treat yourself, don't you?"

"You know I do."

Smiling and shaking my head, I asked her about hair and makeup. She reassures me all will be in place. She asks Ezra, "What time does London need to be ready by on Saturday?"

"The car is picking us up at 6:30. I will let V know to get a plus one and to inform the team you will be attending with me."

I look over at Ezra and when he meets my eyes, I tell him, "Honey, I don't have to walk the carpet with you. I can just go as your guest and go inside and mingle while you do the carpet. I'm okay with keeping a low profile if you don't want this relationship public yet." I want him to have the option of choosing when the public learns about us. I don't feel like he is hiding me, but I know once it is out there it will be a media circus and I don't know if I am ready for that. It's such a weird thought to have so many media outlets involved in our relationship. I have been able to keep my jealous thoughts at bay, but if they start comparing me to past women seen with him, or making images look like more than they are, it will really shake my confidence. I am completely in love with Ezra Everest; I haven't told him that, but I know deep in my bones that I love him. I don't want my insecurities or the media to ruin this for us.

While holding my gaze, he sincerely tells me, "London, I am ready for the media circus that will come with us being public. I have been waiting a long time for you, and I don't care who knows that I found you."

"Awwwww." We both looked to the side and see Amelia staring at us. "That was so sweet. London, you don't say no to an answer like that." Amelia has never had a filter, and it is still missing all these years later. She thinks it, she says it. Got to love her unadulterated honesty.

I turn and wrap my arms around his neck and slide in closer to give him the sexiest kiss I can manage because Ami is right. You don't say no to a man who uses words like that. After coming up for air, I say against his lips, "I'll be beside you through everything as long as you'll have me."

Chapter Eleven

After one more meeting with law enforcement and strong advisement to them that all other inquiries can be handled through our legal teams, the police stop contacting us. I believe it helps that the medical examiner's report determined the cause of death as suicide. After getting the notification from our legal team about the ME report, Ezra and I took a moment and prayed for that poor girl's soul to find peace. We also anonymously send a very large bouquet of flowers to her family and have Amelia find out when the funeral service is to send a funeral arrangement as well. The sorrow that family is feeling right now is very familiar to me, but hopefully, the flowers will provide a small form of joy to remember all the good memories they shared with their loved one.

The sorrow I see in Ezra's eyes while I am ordering the flowers shows just how empathic this man is and I fall in love with him even more. I have been wrestling with myself about saying the words to him. I know he sees it in my actions, but saying the words feels different. I have been so in my head about it. Is it too soon? Will I scare him away? Does he feel the same? Why am I so scared to say the words? What if he doesn't feel how I feel? There are so many questions and so much second-guessing in my head. I know what my heart feels and what my head knows. I know that my soul feels complete, so why am I not shouting 'I love you' every time I catch him watching me or every time he comes into a room and kisses me? His thoughtfulness, his touches, his listening ear, his advice, his encouragement, his bad jokes, his good jokes, his beautiful eyes, his smile, his empathy, his compassion, his tongue, the earth-shattering sex, the way he holds me at night, the way he watches me, and the flowers … how can I not tell him? I have to say the words; they are so close to just falling out, but I really want it to be a good moment, not while we are both still working through the trauma of finding a dead body and of me reliving Piper's death.

But I made my decision. I will tell him, and even if he doesn't say it back, I want him to know, and isn't it better for me to know now if he doesn't feel the same? I don't know if my heart would recover, but I have other things in my life that would keep me busy, and I would eventually bounce back.

Having made my decision, I can focus on the dresses that Amelia has laid out in front of me. Amelia has been quiet this morning while we view dresses, and she is doing work at the hotel. Tired of the silence, I ask, "Ami, is everything alright? You're quiet this morning. All this fashion usually has you buzzing."

Closing her laptop, she says, "I was just giving you the space you needed to get out of your head. You looked deep in thought when you came in. Want to talk about it?"

"No need, I worked it out," I say with a sincere smile because Amelia really is my best friend. She knows exactly what I need without even asking. "You know me so well, Amelia. I think I'll keep you around."

"Ha, you'd better. I know where the bodies are." We both laugh as we let the glitz and glamor of fashion fill our morning.

Amelia found a local up-and-coming designer in San Bernadino who brought the most stylish and stunning dresses I have ever seen. I shouldn't call them dresses because they're more like works of art. The designer, Rain, is here with her best friend and assistant, Tempe, to help me pick a dress.

I tried on several dresses. They are each equally stunning, but as I model them for Amelia and the designer, they veto several that I love. Some we both agreed when I tried them on: not a good color, not flashy enough, does nothing for your figure, too revealing for my taste.

It seems like we've gone through everything until Tempe comes back into the suite with another bag. Rain quickly says to Tempe, "No, she won't like that, it's not—" Tempe gives Rain a side-eye that stops her from what she is about to say.

Tempe then looks at me. "This is a brand-new idea Rain had about a week ago. She's just nervous because it's not her usual style of design. I think you should try it on. It will be perfect for this event."

I look over at Rain, who is trying to open a hole in the floor to swallow her with her eyes. I can see how nervous she is about this piece. I say, "Rain, everything you have shown me is beautiful. I'm sure this dress will be the showstopper we're looking for."

Rain picks up her head, pushes her shoulders back, and says, "Okay, let's try it."

I am happy to see her regain her confidence. Nothing is scarier than stepping out of your comfort zone. Tempe opens the dress bag, and a mint-colored masterpiece is displayed. Amelia and I both gasp.

I turn to Rain and say, "I can't wear that; it should be in a museum somewhere! What if dirt gets on it? This is too beautiful for me. I am not the person you want in this dress. You need a real celebrity to debut this. Wow, girl. Just OMG."

I can't believe Rain was nervous about showing this dress; it looks so perfect. I can see relief in her eyes that I like it. After taking a deep breath, she says, "It would be my honor for you to wear this. I think you are the perfect woman for this dress."

"Rain, wow, okay, yes. I will do my best to make this dress turn every head." I am so honored she would let me wear her most recent design, but not only that, something that she feels is a risk to take in her industry and for her brand. "Let's try it on."

Chapter Twelve

The day of the premiere comes in a hurry, and it feels like I am a part of some professional production or a major athletic event. Because Ezra doesn't like vendors knowing his actual home address, Amelia has arranged for us to get ready in a glamorous suite at the famous Beverly Hotel. She has rented one of their villas for us to have privacy and fun while getting ready. Ezra and I checked in last night, or rather I checked in and he came to the room after security took him through the private entrance. Amelia booked the room with my information to keep the press from knowing where he is. Ezra and I had the most romantic evening: food that looked like art and tasted like heaven, the best champagne I have ever tasted, and sex on multiple surfaces in this room. I woke up refreshed and sore in all the right places.

Amelia and I make the best team. She calls at 5 a.m. to wake me and I snooze until 5:45, which she expects, and then she's making her way into the suite by 6 a.m. with coffee and our plan for all of today's preparation events. While she is setting up coffee and breakfast, Ezra and I have a shower that should be illegal; we both come in a hot, fast, and muffled rush before he exits the shower while I wash my hair. After last night, you would think he'd be spent, but that man has the stamina of a mustang, which works for me just fine.

I walk into the living area to find Ezra and Amelia laughing about something and Ezra stuffing his mouth with food.

"Good morning. What are y'all laughing at this early in the morning?" I ask as I make my way to a coffee mug.

Amelia responds with, "The fact that y'all think your shower sex was quiet. London, you come loudly even 'quietly,' and I was congratulating Ezra on the fact that he actually knows how to make you come. You know, he's not just a pretty face. I shocked him with my bluntness, he choked a bit on his food, and we laughed."

I smile because Amelia has caught me up on the conversation before I can finish making my coffee and Ezra gets a real view of my best friend. I am so happy she is finally more comfortable with him because if Ami is talking about sex with you, it means you are on track to be her friend. That girl has a dirty mind, and we often laugh about my sex life or hers.

Instead of trying to change the subject to see if it will make Ezra more comfortable, I lean into the conversation as if this is any other morning with Ami. "Well, he does give good orgasms, as in multiple. I haven't found better. I think I'll keep him."

"Multiple orgasms, London? Fucking marry him when he asks." Both of us laugh at that because neither of us has ever discussed getting married before.

Ezra chimes in without shying away. "So, being able to give multiple orgasms makes me husband material? I will be sure to add that to the 'man guide' because I'm betting they don't know that."

"That's a pricy secret to give away," I say. "Be sure you trademark it."

"Oh no, this 'man guide' is for us all. No one gets to claim it."

Amelia adds, "I have a few more gems for this guide. I'll send you the PDF."

Ezra laughs. He kisses me on the month with joy in his eyes. It sends tingles all through me. "I'm going to be out for a few hours," he says. "I've got to go to the barber and make a few media stops before coming back here to get dressed. My arrival time at the event is at 7:15 p.m. and I have a minimum of forty minutes of red carpet before I can go inside the theater."

Amelia jumps in with, "She will be ready to leave no later than 6:15 p.m. V sent me the list of press you'll be doing and approved comments for London to make. With the event that happened at your condo, some press already have her name, so I imagine tonight will be filled with questions about the relationship instead of the movie, but I have all the things for London to say to make sure the focus stays on the film."

"Looks like I will be prepared for your red carpet, Mr. Everest," I say. "Don't you worry, by the time I'm finished, I will be ready to be on your arm or cheering in the corner for the mega-star 'The Mountain' himself. I'll be sure I'm ready to make you shine. As they say, 'teamwork makes the dream work.' And this team, you and me, we work."

I kissed him again. He shakes his head at the People magazine nickname the press often refers to him as and adds, "This team does work." The way he says it lifts my heart because it is like he is vocalizing his love without saying those three words. His words clicked in my head; we have been through something horrible and come out on the other side stronger. This team works. Our love, it works. Ezra and I have the foundation to build a life-long love and I intend to pull my weight in this team.

After he leaves, it feels like I am shining from the inside out because there is nothing that can rain on this day. I get to wear a beautiful dress and experience Ezra in his work, his art, and as a major part of his life. This day is the dream of many women, and I get to live it.

Amelia is already in motion, with a phone in one hand and her laptop in front of her, when the first knock comes at the door.

"That will be the mani/pedi arriving now," she says as she walks to the door while typing out a text or email. She is in multi-tasker mode and could be doing many things with her phone right now.

The nail techs set up as Amelia and I discuss today's schedule and the Nebraska project that I will be leaving for tomorrow. We have to go to Nebraska to get started on this project and to get settled; we will be living there for at least the next eight months, although the project is scheduled to last for two years.

While I am getting my manicure and pedicure, Amelia and I have a video meeting with Elle to discuss the final stages of the South Carolina project, the start of the Nebraska project, and putting out the job announcement for a new assistant. Because with two projects going, even if South Carolina is wrapping, Elle and Ami will need help.

Before wrapping up the call, Elle suggests, "London, I hope it's okay, but Ami shared with me who you're dating and what happened in L.A. I have signed all the non-disclosure agreements from Danielle."

"Me too," Ami adds before Elle continues.

"I think we should ask V for a recommendation on the assistant, just because we will need someone who can travel and be discreet with anything he or she may see when it comes to," she hesitates because she knows we are not alone right now, "the ocean floor." She laughs at her horrible attempt at a code name, and Ami and I laugh too.

"The ocean floor?" Ami looks amused and puzzled.

"Yeah, you know, impossible depth and definitely magical. That's what I would think if I was swimming in it." Elle laughs at herself. She fits in so perfectly with us.

Ami continues with, "Yeah, I'm sure London is riding in the deep very well."

"And drowning multiple times a day has never felt so good," I throw in as they both laugh hysterically.

"I didn't know that Danielle asked you both for non-disclosures," I say after we've calmed down, a bit disappointed that Danielle didn't trust my judgment when it came to my staff. "I wouldn't have asked y'all to sign those."

Amelia can see my disappointment and says, "It has nothing to do with your judgment of character or our ability to be discreet. It's about protecting 'the ocean floor.' London, you care about him, and we care about you, so we signed those documents to ensure your happiness."

That was such a sweet and true friend move. I knew I made the perfect choice with Ami as my right hand, but having Elle agree with Ami shows that hiring Elle was also the right move.

"Thanks," I tell them. "I don't want this relationship to change our work or our friendships. We still need to run this business smoothly and without any unnecessary challenges because of 'the ocean floor.'" This code name is here to stay, obviously. "If you think V has some options for assistants then we will take recommendations, but the three of us have the final say in who we hire. We will not add someone to this team who will stop our progression or cause a rift in our work ethic. So, take the recs from V, but also reach out to some temp agencies and head-hunters with the position. We will interview and get the ball rolling. Sooner rather than later; I don't want you, me, or Elle to be overwhelmed with small tasks that are best to delegate."

We end the call, with everyone having their to-do lists, just as the nail techs are finishing my mani/pedi.

The day continues with more knocks at the door and more pampering for this event. Ami and I work through most of the services, answering emails and taking conference calls. After lunch, we have massages that are quiet and relaxing, just as they were intended to be. Once the massages are finished, we have an hour before hair and makeup arrive, so we spend it working with Elle on speakerphone.

By 5:30 p.m., hair and makeup are done. Rain and Tempe arrive with the dress, shoes, and accessories. The makeup assistant stays behind for touch-ups; she will even be on the red carpet to make sure I am ready for photos and videos.

Tempe will also go with us to the carpet to make sure the dress is perfect in all photos.

As I am opening a bottle of wine and picking at the small snacks the hotel has brought in for us this evening, Ezra comes back. He enters quietly and I don't even hear him when he comes into the suite. No one does, because we all look up shocked when he says, "Evening, ladies."

Rain, Tempe, and the makeup assistant are star-struck and can't say a word. I smirk, shaking my head, and Ami laughs at their open-mouthed expression before saying, "Pull it together, ladies, he only said hello."

They all come out of their moment to say, "Hello," "Hi," and "Hey," in unison.

Ezra walks over to me and kisses me right on the mouth in front of everyone. It is a long, lingering kiss with tongue and it should make me blush in front of a room full of women who are obviously his fans, but it doesn't. This kiss is the same way he has greeted me every time he comes home from work and sees me in the kitchen or living room, and now I can add hotel suite to that list.

"Hey, how did you win today?" is the first thing I have said to him when he comes in after work for the last few weeks we have been living in the same house. He always gives me a good answer or a dirty answer, but since we are around company now, he says, "Got ahead of a few nasty stories today, met with Rose, and was at the community center to help some local kids with their acting. Today was good."

There is a sign over our shoulder and we both look to find the rest of the women staring at us. I am laughing when I say, "I believe your fan pool just got bigger."

He sees me looking over his shoulder and kisses my lips once more before leaving the room, saying, "Bye, ladies."

They all say, "Bye," in unison again. After ogling him as he walks away, they turn back to me, snap out of it, and jump into action. The makeup assistant fixes my lips and the highlighter that smudged with that kiss and Rain tells me she is ready to get me in the dress.

Of course, Ezra is ready twelve minutes after he gets out of the shower. He comes out of the bathroom in his tux with cufflinks in his hand. He watches Ami, Rain, and Tempe strap me into the dress.

"That color is amazing on you, honey," he says from the other side of the room.

Rain says, "Thanks," before I can tell him about it being a special design that Rain is very nervous about showing the world. Rain stands beside me to finish closing the dress and when Tempe sees Ezra struggling to get his cufflinks closed, she goes over and starts to help him finish, taking the cufflinks and fixing his tie without him asking for help. I don't even think she notices that she has done it, because fashion is her life, and she wants to make sure everyone looks their best to feel their best.

She is doing a walk around when she notices something. "Mr. Everest, your hem in the back of the pants has dropped a few stitches and the jacket needs to come in a bit," she says. "Can I fix them?"

She is already walking to her kit before he can answer her. I believe she is going to fix it no matter what; this dress is perfection, and she will not let him ruin its debut. Ezra looks at the jacket and pant leg and says, "Yes," just as Tempe is getting down to fix the hem. She is done in less than a minute with the leg and then pins the jacket the way she wants before asking him to take it off. It took her about five minutes to finish the jacket and we both turned around to see each other at the same time.

"Wow, baby, you should wear a tux every day," I say. "That is a look for you. Like the kind that gets you special oral jobs."

Ezra's eyes shot up to my face from their slow climb to take in the dress. "I like oral jobs," is all he says before he gives me the spin sign and I turn for him in this show-stopping dress.

The color is the eye-catcher, and with the soft clinging lines, the side cutout, the off-the-shoulder strap, the small train, and the bustled bottom, this dress is a dream. "London, I have no words," he says. "That dress was made for you. Stunning, sexy, and alluring. Knowing I get to take it off you later is the best part."

Ami jumps in to add, "Wow, you two have the most alluring sexual chemistry, but tone it down if you don't want the world in your business after this red carpet." We both look at her like she is crazy as she continues, "And you are both beautiful people who look beyond amazing right now."
I pull Ami into a hug because she is my favorite. I grabbed Ezra's phone and opened the camera to snap a selfie of Ami and me, then handed him his phone back. He gets behind us and takes another. Ezra hands Ami his camera, asking, "Take a photo of us before the madness." Ami takes a few shots and Rain and Tempe keep pulling and fixing the dress.

"It's perfect, Rain," I assure her. "I'm manifesting that you will be overflowing with special orders and style consultations after this event. I will be dropping your name like 'rain' all night." I laugh at my own pun as everyone shakes their head. "Oh, come on, that was funny," I say. "Rain all night, because her name is Rain."

Rain is smiling when she says, "Oh, we got the joke, London, but that doesn't change how corny it was."

"Corny, funny, same thing."

Ezra leads me to the front room where Sara, the makeup assistant, stops in her tracks before saying, "Whoa, that dress, just whoa. You both look crazy amazing." She grabs a kit and adds a bit of color to my eyes and lightens my lipstick shade. Then they leave, on their way to the venue for last-minute touchups before photos.

At exactly 6 p.m. a blacked-out Range Rover arrives at the villa, and we leave via a private exit. Getting in the car is easy, but I am worried about getting out, especially without help.

Ezra has closed the privacy window and he leans into my ear to whisper, "Oral favors in this dress are a must, but you can't make a sound. Can you do that, London?" he asks as he turns me and lowers himself under the dress.

"Baby, I don't think you can get there in this. I am in here pretty securely."

But Ezra Everest has never met a mountain he couldn't climb, because that man eats me like a champion and drinks down my silent, seat clenching, window prints climax without ruining my dress. I am catching my breath when he comes out from under my dress, saying, "Very good, London. You didn't make a sound and we didn't ruin your hairstyle or dress. You look thoroughly fucked and blushed from my mouth. I will get to taste you on my lips as we walk this carpet together, hand in hand." When he gets himself seated again, he reaches into his jacket pocket to get a handkerchief and ensures he doesn't have my climax shining around his mouth.

I don't get to recover or ask more questions before the driver stops. There is a knock on Ezra's door and then it is opened. The crowd goes wild when Ezra steps out of the car. I see his hand go up and wave as he turns back to me and says, "Let go, baby," and reaches his hand in to take mine. I have just enough time to give myself a four-phrase mental pep talk: "Shoulders back, head up, smile, you are enough."

As I exit the car, the crowd is still going wild and yelling Ezra's name. He is smiling and waving, and then his eyes lock on mine as if to say, "Let me show you my world." I can't take my eyes off his, but I feel Tempe appear out of what seems like nowhere, fixing the dress at the back and bottom while Sara, also appears at my side, they arrived ahead of us and used the crew passes to be at our car when we exited. Sara turns my head slightly to retouch my lipstick and then says, "Show me your smile," which I do. "No lipstick; good to go."

That's all Ezra needs to hear because he pulls my hand to lead me down the carpet. We stop and pose for pictures. I am stiff to begin with, and I know Ezra notices because he leans in to whisper, "Relax or we will have to go in the bathroom for another round of oral treatment for you, and it will make us late for the movie."

I lean in to listen to him, thinking he is about to tell me where he wants me to stand or how to move, not expecting a dirty comment. I slowly lean back and give him a sultry stare that tells him how much I enjoyed my treatment and how I can't wait for the next one, and then I smirk a bit and say with sarcasm, "Oh no, we wouldn't want that now, would we? Oh, the scandal that would cause."

He turns his smile up 100 watts and discreetly pats my ass before turning back to the cameras, but I can't take my eyes off him. He is working the carpet and has managed to get me to relax for the photos. He tells me which way to focus my eyes and not to look at the flash on any of the cameras. We work through poses, and I do the ones Ami and I practiced that best show off the dress without taking the spotlight off Ezra. Tempe comes in a few times to rearrange the dress and fix Ezra's sleeve and then disappears again. I keep wondering where she is going, but Ezra keeps us moving down the carpet. I hear a few photographers yell, "Ezra, can we get you alone?"

I lift the back of my dress and move to step back, but he says, "Don't leave. Together, remember? We're a team."

My heart melts at that. It is at this moment that I realize I am overwhelmed with the love this man shows me. I look forward to smile at the cameras but feel him watching me while I pose for the photos.

Tempe is fixing my dress again as we make our way to the next 'X' on the carpet to pose. Ezra hasn't stopped touching me all night; every moment he has been leading and holding me through this madness that is his career. When he tucks a strand of my hair back into its style, I can't help myself. I lean into his ear to very quietly whisper, "I am in love with you."

I make sure my mouth is covered, to speak very low, and that I am close enough to his ear when I speak the words. Ami was adamant with her instruction on how to talk with Ezra while all the cameras are flashing and videos going. I can still hear her saying, "Lean in close to talk, cover your mouth to the best of your ability, whisper, and when possible, speak into his ear." I can tell that my words catch him off-guard and his grip on my hip tightens, but his outward expression doesn't falter. He is trained to ensure that these people don't get to see the real him; only those close to him know his real smile and the real Ezra. I get the real him and it makes me love him even more. I love us, this team, this man.

He can't respond to what I've said right now and I know that, but I look him in the eye, and a moment passes before we both turn back to the cameras.

We finish the carpet and then head to the TV media row of cameras to give comments. This part is much less stressful for me because the plan is for me to step out and let Ezra handle the TV row alone, but he doesn't let go of my hand as he heads for the first camera, and he keeps holding my hand through every brief interview. By the time we get to the fifth camera, he has his arm securely around my waist and his fingers on the top of my ass. His body language is saying 'Don't you dare leave,' and I am listening to his body. This is the sexual chemistry that Ami was talking about and I am so turned on right now by the glances and discreet touches, but I think Ezra may be coming to his end and wants alone time. All the TV personalities are asking who I am to him, and he effectively avoids the question and keeps the conversation on the movie. But I don't know if he slipped or if he was waiting to get to a reporter named Liza because when she asks, "Ezra, the body language and the chemistry coming off you two right now, this must be your girlfriend. How long have you been together?" he responds.

He looks at me when he answers. "I feel like I have been with London forever, but officially it has only been three months."

I correct him and say, "Four," and Liza looks at me with genuine happiness in her eyes for me and Ezra.

"Four months, Ezra, get it right," she says to him, then adds, "You are a beautiful couple. We all wish you happiness."

I don't know if Ezra gave her a signal or what because the next thing I know she is looking at the camera and going back to the studio, and we are done with TV and being moved to a different location. Ezra looks me in the eyes and says, "Wait here and don't move. I want to sign some autographs for the fans. Don't leave, London."

I look up at him, thinking why would I move? but I just say "Okay, waiting here."

I watch as he enters the crowd with some security officers. He poses for selfies and signs autographs. Several people with earpieces asked me to move on or stand to the side but I politely declined and stayed in the spot that Ezra wanted me to wait in. After several more pictures, he checks over his shoulder and looks directly at me. He signs a few more autographs and then waves goodbye to everyone as they continue to scream his name. He walks right back to me and links our fingers before leading me into a room that is all white and completely quiet.

"Where are we now?" I ask.

"Waiting room, until they're ready to lead you to our seats and then they will announce me, and I will join you. Say it again."

"Say what again?" I think I know what he wants to hear but I don't want to assume.

"Say it again, London," is all he says.

"I am in love with you."

He pushes us up against the wall, blocks me in, and leans his forehead against mine. He takes a deep breath and speaks softly as if he's trying not to be overhead.

"This wasn't too much; it didn't scare you off," he says. "This is my career and I really do love it. I don't want to stop anytime soon. There will be many of these events throughout our life. You don't have to come to all of them, but I will want you at a lot of them. Are you sure? Because I have loved you since the day I left North Carolina and realized I never wanted to be without you again. I think maybe I loved you even before then, but I didn't want to scare you off with the depth of my feelings. London …" He exhales deeply and continues quietly, "I am in love with you too."

The smile on my face should tell him everything, but I say softly too, "I felt your love, Ezra, even when you didn't say it. This isn't too much. I am so incredibly proud of you and of being on your arm. All your hard work to get to this point in your career. All the no's you overcame, all the negative comments, all the struggles you endured. You deserve this. You earned it. Our life will be what we make it. I am overjoyed that you would choose me to be on your team and that you would share your life with me. I will be a good teammate. Your love, your trust, your dreams, and your loyalty are what I want, and I will work daily to keep them."

He kisses me deeply and leans his hips against mine, so I know how my words have affected him. There are two knocks on the door, and he slows and stops the kiss before knocking back once. A lady enters the room and says, "We are ready to take you to your seat, Ms. Isle. They are ready for you, Mr. Everest."

Ezra nods and the lady leaves again. He looks at me and kisses me softly. "Do I have lipstick on me?" he asks with a smile.

I check him out. "No, you're perfect."

He slides his hand over my bare shoulder and down the exposed side of my dress before squeezing my ass and kissing my shoulder. "Fuck, I want you so bad right now. We are not staying for the whole movie."

I straighten his jacket and say, "Yes, dear. I'll tell Ami to have a car ready."

"You do that, London, because when we get home, I have a mountain for you to slide down."

"I like the way you think, Everest," is all I say before two men arrive, one for me and one for him. They lead us in separate directions. All I can think is that I can't wait to ride him, and that he loves me back.

Chapter Thirteen

We only stayed for the first forty-five minutes of the movie. Ezra can't wait to get me home and when the attendant comes to our seat to escort us out, I am nearly running to keep up with him in these heels. I have to ask him to slow down twice before he threatens to carry me if I don't keep up. I am inwardly swooning at how sexually charged he is about us finally saying 'I love you' to each other. He's ready to carry me caveman style to his lair and have his way with me. The car ride is full of sexual charge too. I stroke his thigh and dick the whole way, while he has his hand on my thigh and his head resting back as he enjoys my touch.

He stills my hand as we get closer to the house and I pick up the speed of my strokes. He kisses my shoulder and whispers in my ear so Dein can't hear, "I will not come in my tux, London. You promised me oral care in this tux. I intend to come in your mouth and then in that tight pussy. Hands to yourself for now." He kisses my neck and then leans his head back, taking a deep breath as if to steady himself before we get to the house.

We pull into the garage and Ezra tells Dein, "That will be all tonight, Dein. Is the house empty?"

"As requested, Ezra. I will see you tomorrow to drive London to the airport," Dein says, and we exit the car.

We enter the house, and it is lit with candlelight and there are ranunculi on every surface leading to the bedroom. It is straight out of a romance novel and breathtaking to see. "Ezra, this is perfect. Your flower selection continues to get me wet."

"I only select them with getting you wet in mind," he says, standing directly behind me as I take in the space. He leans down to kiss my neck and trace my shoulder with his tongue. A shiver runs up my back. This man always knows where to put his mouth to turn on the waterfall in my panties. We are so connected and now that I know he loves me too, this lovemaking is going to be on another level.

"I love that you always give me flowers, Ezra." I exhale with a sigh as he unzips my dress and takes off his jacket.

"I loved having you next to me on the red carpet tonight. It took all my strength not to walk it with a hard dick knowing that I am the only one who gets to undress you tonight and every night," he whispers as he undoes his tie and pushes the dress off my body. I step out of the dress, and I am left in the jewelry, a sexy bra, and high heels.

"Fuck, London, I love when you don't wear panties."

"I'll do it more often for you. I've been fantasizing all evening about you eating my pussy in these heels with my legs over your shoulders. That's what I was thinking about while you walked next to me on the red carpet, that and how in love I am with you."

That is all it takes for him to speed things up because he is moaning on my shoulder when he wraps his arm around me, turns me around, and begins to devour my mouth. This is the kiss of a man on a mission. This is Ezra's kiss, the one that says he loves me and is about to fuck my back out. He moves me to the entryway's high table and pushes me to sit on it before kneeling in front of me. He licks his way up my leg and my breathing has already increased. "Babe, this table will not withstand this," I warned him.

"I don't give a fuck. You talk like that, you get what you want." His hands grip my calves and he puts one heeled leg over his shoulder, just as I imagined he would, and then he spreads the other leg wide so he has a full view of my center. He uses his strength to pull me to the edge of the table and holds me there while he looks at me. He's close enough to my pussy that I can feel his breath.

"London, you are already so wet for me. Your pussy is weeping."

I moan at his words. He is so close that I can feel his lips moving while he talks. "Ezra, please," is all I can get out before he kisses me exactly where I want. "Oh Ezra, yes," I say as my head falls back against the wall and my hands clamp down on the side of the table, trying to help hold myself up to keep us both from falling.

He stops long enough to say, "Watch me, London. Watch how fucking hot it is with my mouth in your pussy and these sexy as fuck shoes on my shoulder. You look like a fucking goddess right now, so open for me and needy."

I do as he says and watch him as he licks, kisses, and uses his tongue to bring me to climax. My orgasm hits like a freight train as I scream his name and try to close my legs, but Ezra is not having it. "Come again," is what I hear in the muted bliss of my orgasm.

"I can't."

"You fucking can. Come again." His words and his tongue work because before I know it, I am drenching his face again with my cum and pulling his head back because it is too much. I will not pass out before I feel his cock in me. I am trying to slow my breathing and he is kissing his way up my body and then we are moving again with my legs around his waist. Because, let's face it, my legs are useless right now after two of the most powerful orgasms ever. He sits on the foyer lounge chair with me on top and manages to work his pants down far enough to get his cock out and me on it. I slide down on him and we are face-to-face, nose-to-nose, eye-to-eye, breathing the same air, so completely connected. Sex has never been like this with anyone else, and I can never get enough of the intimacy this man gives me. He listens when I speak, and he touches me in all the right places, both inside and outside. He has my best interests at heart and makes me a better woman; I want to be the best woman for him. This moment is so powerful, every moment we are this connected is so powerful, but the love I am feeling right now is otherworldly. Maybe it is because we said the words, or maybe it is just us. I don't care what it is; I just know that I don't ever want to lose this. I don't ever want to lose him.

"I love you, Ezra. All of you," I whisper in this moment of closeness without breaking eye contact.

"I love you, London. With everything I am."

I begin to rock up and down and around and he drops his hands to my ass as he guides me to ride his cock. He is so big, and, in this position, I can feel all of him. The hurt is so good, and he is so deep. Our lips are connected, and the kiss is a slow, dirty, and tongue-filled form of ecstasy. I can still taste myself on his lips and tongue and it is heightening my arousal. He moans in my mouth, "Baby, yes, fuck, just like that." His words are all the encouragement I need to speed up my strokes.

"Knees up," he moans into my shoulder, where he is licking and biting me.

I groan at his directions because his voice is such an aphrodisiac. I do as requested, and my strokes are faster, and he is lifting his hips to meet me and watching as his cock enters me. His eyes are so hooded, and it is the sexiest thing I have seen. Watching him watch us have sex. I can't help my words. "Fuck, Ezra."

"That's it, London, come on. Take me. All of me. My cock is weeping for your tight pussy. He was made for you. I'm going to come in you." He is saying all the dirty things while watching my pussy take his dick.

I know he's getting closer because his grip on my ass is getting tighter, his hips are meeting mine faster, and he's biting his lip. He keeps his hips going as he looks up at me to see the sheer ecstasy on my face and then he watches where we are connected and exhales loudly. "London," is all he can get out before he uses his fingers to find my clit. "I need you to come with me, baby. You can do it."

I am nodding as his finger pressure gets stronger on my clit. He is coaching and telling me how sexy I am right now riding his cock, telling me how close he is and how good it is going to feel for him to come inside me. "Oh god, Ezra," and just like that, I am falling over the edge again and he is right along with me, with a loud curse and a shout of my name.

We are both catching our breath when I look around and notice we had sex right in front of the main door of the house. It's a good thing he doesn't have neighbors. It was so hot, and we're surrounded by the beautiful flowers he got for me and filled with the love we share.

"Wow, that was stellar," I say.

He laughs. "Stellar, huh?"

"Oh god, yes. I don't know if I have the power to lift off you. How are you still dressed?"

"That vision you had put me over the edge, babe. I had to have you."

I lay my head in the crook of his neck and kiss his sexy jawline. "It was such a vivid daydream while we walked the carpet. I thought it was best I shared it with you. Being that we share dreams now."

"And I am so glad you shared."

"Let's get your clothes off and shower. I still owe you a blow job that will roll your eyes back." I stand up and off him. He watches as his cum starts traveling down my inner thigh and he uses his fingers to rub it back against me and then puts those fingers inside me.

"That is exactly what I was thinking," he says with a smile as he pumps his finger inside of me and then stands. We kiss and touch and rub and we manage to make it in the shower, leaving a trail of his clothes, shoes, and jewelry on our way to the bathroom. Tonight is going to be a long, hot, sweaty, sexy, and loving night.

Chapter Fourteen

Our goodbyes are getting harder, but Ezra is doing everything he can to reassure me that we will be fine. We have sexy soul-lifting sex early in the morning, mid-morning, and thirty minutes before I have to leave for the airport. We link calendars and set travel dates. This long-distance thing will be a piece of cake and hopefully will not feel like long distance at all. But all that won't make not sleeping in the same bed and not kissing him on the way out the door in the morning any easier.

The ride to the airport is mostly quiet. I can still feel the way his mouth feels on me and the effects of the hard and fast sex we had in the doorway before walking out to meet the car.

"Ezra, baby, I am really going to miss you."

"Me too, honey. But it's only five days before I'm in Nebraska for a while with you. This works, we work, and we will always be sure we are making it work. Distance doesn't stop this."

I slide closer and kiss him deeply because he is right, this will be hard work, but that saying has never been more relevant than right now. Nothing worth it is easy, and this, what we have, is worth it. Instead of making this a tearful 'see you soon,'

I am going to trust us. Without removing my lips from his, I murmur, "You say the sweetest things, Ezra Everest."

"You should definitely keep me around because my mouth game is fire."

I laugh because he is so right; that tongue and lips of his are life-altering. "In so many ways."

With one last kiss, we pulled into the private entrance for LAX. He wanted to be able to walk in with me, so V arranged for a private arrival. It's just another reason I love him, and I know this will work.

We sit in the car and make out until there is no choice but to get out or I won't make it through security in time to catch my flight.

"I love you and I will see you in a few days, babe," is the last thing on his lips as I go through security and head to my gate.

I met Amelia at boarding. We are on the same flight, and she gives me a sad smile before saying, "We will be so busy that these five days will fly by, and then you'll be picking him up at the airport." I smile at her because she is always here when I need her the most.

* * * *

Amelia is right; we are so busy these next five days in Nebraska, setting up and settling into our rental, that I don't notice the days that Ezra and I are apart. Ezra and I talk daily and text, which makes the time apart not only shorter but sexier too. When it's time to pick him up from the airport, I can't get him to the house fast enough to do dirty things to him. The time apart only makes us love each other more and the 'see you soon' is easier because we have committed to each other. No, we don't want to be apart, but we are committed to this relationship and the love that we have.

Our routine is working and by the time Ezra has to travel to set to be on location for a new film, I am able to go with him because of the team I have in place. I can work from anywhere and my team makes it easy to trust them and know that things will get done.

* * * *

We are in Cairo, Egypt, for the month, and the time change has been messing up my body's internal clock. I'm working from the hotel when Amelia reminds me of my evening schedule, which includes a pyramid tour with Ezra.

"Ami, can we reschedule the tour? I am not feeling being in all that dirt and it will be dark. How much of the pyramids can we see in the dark?" I ask. Ami and Elle say, 'No,' at the same time with so much force. Jeez is all I can think. "Wow, I'm sure it's not that serious, and Ezra would be cool with dinner in the room."

Elle chimes in with, "Where's your sense of adventure, London? You're in Cairo. Do the tour."

Ami says, "You can sleep when you're dead." I laugh at them because obviously, they want me to go on this tour. "And it cost a lot of money and effort for me to arrange a private tour for you and the ocean floor," Ami adds, because we are still using code names for some reason when we talk about Ezra, "from across all these time zones."

I shake my head at the screen. "I'm sure V did all the heavy lifting, Ami."

"Whatever. Go on the fucking tour."

"Yes, go, London," Elle agrees.

"Fine, I will go on the fucking tour. Let me go then so I can get ready and pull some energy from somewhere."

"Yes, get ready and wear something cool and sexy."

"Ugh, now I have to try with my outfit. You didn't say all that. I was going to wear leggings and a T-shirt."

Again, they say in unison, "No." Ami adds, "Try harder."

"Fine. Bye."

"We love you," is what I hear as I leave the video call.

Try harder. Why do I need to try harder? It will be just me, Ezra, and the tour guide, I imagine.

* * * *

When Ezra comes home from shooting, he is still covered in stunt makeup and looking tired. I offer, "Baby, if you want to cancel the tour, I'm okay with it. We can do a Netflix and chill kind of night."

He comes into the room to see me standing in front of the closet in my underwear and says, "What, no. I'm fine. I will shower and get ready." He doesn't forget to kiss me before he goes to shower. He never forgets to kiss me when he gets home.

After our kiss, I'm still trying to give him an out. "Are you sure? Don't rally for me. Matter of fact…" I walk up to him and kiss him softly on the neck and jawline, "I can help you relax," kiss, "and then we can pass out in front of Netflix."

I can feel him almost giving in, but then he says, "No. No. This is going to be fun, and my schedule may not allow for a reschedule. You know I don't like to cancel last minute."

He rushes off just as I am about to reach into his pants. I say, "Fine, we'll go," to his dust as he heads into the bathroom.

Try harder is all I can think while getting ready, but my 'try harder' is limited by how tired I am. I found something cute and comfortable and put on my nice sandals; hopefully, we are not doing a lot of walking because I don't want sore feet at the end of this. I am packing a bookbag for us when Ezra comes out dressed casually and sexy. I think I should change. "You look good, baby," I say. "Do I need to change? Is there something happening on this tour? Will there be press?"

"Oh, no, just us. You look great, honey."

I accept his answer because I trust he would never let me show up to anything underdressed. He comes over and takes the packed bookbag from me and we head out for the night. We meet V in the hotel lobby.

"Hey, I have everything set," V says to Ezra as I listen in.

"Thank you, V," we both say, and Ezra adds, "And the dessert?"

"Is perfect, Ez," is all she says to Ezra.

They have such a great relationship that it is not even funny. Watching them together is like watching family. I get the same vibes from these two that I have with Ami. It warms my heart to know Ezra has a good team around him now. Especially with that weasel, William, sidelined and out of the picture.

We're heading for the exit when I turn back to see V smiling. I say, "Good night, V."

"Good night, London."

I look over at Ezra. "Why is she so smiley tonight?"

"I don't know," is the clipped answer I got from Ezra.

The car ride to the location is quiet and Ezra seems a bit off, or maybe nervous. I can't get a read on him.

"What's wrong?" I ask. "I told you we didn't have to go if you didn't want to, Ezra."

"No. I'm fine. What are you talking about?"

"Why are you so quiet? You seem annoyed."

"What? No, I'm fine."

Okay, whatever. I'm not about to keep asking him. If he wants to tell me what is wrong, he will. We pull up to the tour location and they have four-wheelers for us to ride. This will be more fun than I thought. Four-wheelers through the desert, yes, please. The sun is setting, and it will be romantic if Ezra gets out of his mood. Our security and tour guide had a conversation and then they come over to Ezra to give us instructions on safety and rules about four-wheelers.

I am excited. "Babe, can I drive?"

"On the way back," he promises. "You don't know where we're going."

"You do?"

He doesn't answer me, just grabs my hand and leads me to the four-wheelers. This outing is getting weird, and Ezra is being weird too. I just take a deep breath and decide we will have fun if it is the last thing we do.

We rode the four-wheeler right up to the Giza pyramid complex and it's amazing. The sunset in the background and the stunning view of these historic landmarks, it's everything. I am so glad that I came on this tour. There's a picnic set up for us after we finish touring the Pyramid of Khafre. Ezra surprised me with the setup; I didn't see it when we drove up and the tour didn't say it came with food.

"Aww babe, you did a picnic. You do know I am a sure bet, though," I tease him when we get to the blanket with food, flowers, and champagne.

"I like to surprise you every once in a while. Keeps it interesting," he says with a glint in his eye. He always keeps things interesting.

The sun has gone down and the sky is that pretty mixture of twilight, not yet dark but not light anymore either. It's the perfect backdrop after all the amazing history we just saw.

"This is amazing, Ezra. And the history of these pyramids is just so interesting. The universe is a very cool and complicated place. Thank you for arranging this."

"My pleasure," he says, but he doesn't seem sure of himself, and it gets my attention enough to bring my focus to him completely. When I look over, he is already staring at me with what looks like wonder and amazement in his eyes.

"What? Did I say something? Something on my face?" I get a napkin as he breaks into a wide smile.

"London. My life has been good. I am having this kick-ass career that has taken me to some wonderful places."

"Such a blessing, right?"

He keeps going like I didn't interject. "But nothing has compared to meeting you and the feeling my heart has when I see you or when I'm with you. It's like you come into a room and I feel at ease. You say something funny, and I laugh with my whole self. You feel stress and I want to do everything to ease it."

"Baby." I keep jumping in, but he is clearly not finished.

"I want to be a better man for you. I want to deserve you now and in the future. I know how it sounds, but I feel like I was only half-living until I met you. You complete me, London."

I still haven't caught on to what is happening and then he raises up onto one knee and my hand shoots to my mouth, because what the actual fuck is happening, and tears fill my eyes because my heart is filled with joy.

"I know that there is no better life for me than with you. London Isle, marry me?" He opens a black box to reveal the most stunning princess-cut diamond with a band made of more diamonds. The center stone is so clear; it sparkles in the night perfectly. I am shocked and I can't believe I didn't want to come on this tour. He wasn't being quiet earlier; he was nervous or working out what he wanted to say. This is the best night ever and I am so lost in my thoughts that I don't realize that I haven't answered him and that tears of joy are coming down my face.

"Honey, you have to answer," he prompts me.

"Oh. Sorry. Yes. Yes! Of course, I will marry you."

He places the ring on my left ring finger, and I hug him. I take him down to the ground with the force behind the hug and the kisses I am raining on him.

"This is why Amelia and Elle were so pushy about me not canceling tonight," I realize. "They knew?"

"Yes, Amelia helped me pick the ring. I sent her my top three choices. She narrowed it down to two. I had the final say."

I hold the ring out in front of me as I am lying on top of him in the sand, in our perfect moment. "You picked so well. God, I love it and I love you more."

"I love you too. No long engagement, though. Let's get married as soon as possible."

"I can handle that."

I kiss him again and the kiss turns into so much more. Then someone coughs because, clearly, I had forgotten we are not alone. Without moving his mouth from mine, he says, "Let's go, London, I want to get you naked."

I am in complete agreement. We took a few photos and then I can't get him to the four-wheelers fast enough. This man amazes me and surprises me, and I can't wait to spend my life with him. All of my trials and life choices have led me to this man, and I have never been more grateful that our paths have converged. Now we will go through this journey together.

To think, it all started with too much wine, an assistant with the nerve to ask, and one email.

The End.

About the Author

Reneé Nicole grew up in a very small town, Franklinton, North Carolina, north of Raleigh, NC. Nicole, as all her family and friends call her, is a middle child and the best aunt ever (there is a mug that says so). Nicole has lived in a few different cities in the United States, but for now calls Chesapeake, Virginia home. Nicole graduated from college with a degree in criminal justice and received a master's in justice studies. Nicole has spent more than a decade in the criminal justice field, specifically, community corrections, first as a state probation and parole officer and now a federal probation officer. Since no one calls her mom or wife, she holds her 'auntie' title proudly, and spends nights in front of a computer screen writing fictional men that do naughty things that would make anyone blush and badass women who want it and love it.

Nicole learned to love books late in life, after being dragged into reading one of the best trilogies of all time. After which, Nicole fell in love with the power of entertainment through words and imagination. Nicole decided to write what she knew and add a lot of steam. Nicole is excited to change her career path and start providing entertainment to every person who picks up her book. Criminal Justice degree and author, sounds about right.

These days you can find Nicole being a federal probation officer, writing violation reports, doing home checks, collecting drug screens and being in federal court (a day job as some may call it). Also, being a certified florist and a small business owner with my sister/business partner, owning a florist business, Petals of Color. Nicole also loves traveling, good rum and/or wine, being with her parents, siblings and family, binge watching T.V., and poolside chilling, all while daydreaming her next book boyfriend who will lead her to an Oprah's Book Club success level novel and a call from a network to turn her books into film. Because why not? If you are going to reach it, you have to manifest it first. Pray, Manifest, and Do the work, in that order.

Check out Nicole's author pages on Instagram and Facebook, like and follow.